OPEN CITY

New York City, Spring 1999
Number Eight

OPEN CITY BOOKS

The Inaugural Title

LINCOLN PLAZA CINEMAS

Six Screens

63rd Street & Broadway
opposite Lincoln Center
757-2280

OPEN CITY

OPEN CITY

OPEN CITY *is a nonprofit journal of the arts.*
Subscription rate is $32 for four issues; institution rate, $40. Make checks payable to: The Segue Foundation. *Mail to: OPEN CITY, 225 Lafayette Street, Suite 1114, New York, NY 10012. E-mail: ocmagazine@aol.com Web site: www.opencitypress.com*

Special thanks to Nick Stone.

Cover photograph: Piotr Uklanski, *Queens*, 1998,
Courtesy of Gavin Brown's Enterprise, New York City.
Title page photograph: David Robbins

ISBN 1-890447-19-6
ISSN 1089-5523

B. Wurtz : Untitled (life drawing), 1990

CONTRIBUTORS' NOTES

QUANG BAO writes fiction, essays, and reviews and has just completed his first novel. He is co-editing an anthology of gay Asian-American artists and lives in Northampton, Massachusetts.

CAITLIN O'CONNOR CREEVY lives in Chicago. She is a former movie critic for the *Chicago Tribune,* and a contributor to *Personals,* a recent collection of essays.

ADRIAN DANNATT is a writer living in Manhattan and Macilly-en-Villette.

ELIZABETH GAFFNEY is the editor at large of *The Paris Review.* Her translation of *The Pollen Room,* by Zoë Jenny, was published this year by Simon and Schuster. Her short stories have appeared in *The Colorado Review, The Brooklyn Review,* and *The North American Review.* She is working on her first novel.

LIAM GILLICK is an artist living in London and New York City. He is represented by Basilico Fine Arts, Robert Prime, and Schipper & Krome.

MARK GONZALES is one of the most famous professional skateboarders in history. A prolific Bay Area artist and zinester, he exhibits his work at Alleged Fine Arts in New York City. He is the author of two books, entitled *Broken Poems* and *Social Problems.*

MICHAEL HAYES publishes the fortnightly *Phnom Penh Post* with his estranged wife, Kathleen.

BETTINA HUBBY is an artist and writer living in Brooklyn. She has been published in *Pierogi Press,* has shown her work in several New York galleries, and has co-produced a book of drawings called *All the People I Am Are Not Inside Me Yet* with collaborator Professor Cal Clements.

JOYCE JOHNSON is the author of *Minor Characters,* which won the 1983 National Book Critics Circle Award for autobiography. Her other books include the novel *In the Night Café* and *What Lisa Knew: The Truths and Lies of the Steinberg Case.*

FRED LEEBRON's stories have appeared in *Grand Street, TriQuarterly, Ploughshares, Threepenny Review,* and elsewhere. His novels include *Out West* and *Six Figures,* which is forthcoming from Knopf. He teaches at Gettysburg College in Gettysburg, Pennsylvania.

GUY LESSER is the contributing editor of *Madison.* For many years he lived above Harry's Bar, Venice.

SAM LIPSYTE lives in New York City and is the senior editor of *Feed.* His fiction has appeared in *The Quarterly, Nerve,* and *5_Trope.* (The editors apologize for inadvertently omitting this contributor's note from Issue #7, where Sam's story, "Old Soul," appeared.)

GEOFFREY O'BRIEN's most recent books are *The Times Square Story* and *Bardic Deadlines: Reviewing Poetry 1984–95.*

SUSAN PERRY is a freelance writer living in New York City. She has written for *Playboy, Spin*, and other publications.

ELLIOTT PUCKETTE was born in Lexington, Kentucky. She lives and works in New York City, where she is represented by Paul Kasmin Gallery.

DAVID ROBBINS is an artist and writer living in Chicago. His most recent book is a work of fiction, *The Ice Cream Social* (Purple Books/Feature Inc.). His most recent exhibition, "Two or Three Comedies," inaugurated the Suburban, a new gallery in Oak Park, Illinois. He is represented by Feature, Inc., in New York City.

HARVEY SHAPIRO is the author of ten books of poetry, the latest of which is *Selected Poems*, published by Wesleyan University Press. He works as a senior editor at *The New York Times Magazine.*

JEFFREY SKINNER's poems have appeared in *The New Yorker, The Atlantic Monthly, Poetry, The Paris Review*, and other journals. His most recent collection is *The Company of Heaven*, in the Pitt Poetry Series. He serves as editorial consultant for Sarabande Books in Louisville, Kentucky.

RICK SNYDER's poems have recently appeared in *LVNG, Nedge, Hanging Loose*, and *Skanky Possum.* His chapbook, *Blueprint*, is forthcoming from Eight-Eleven Press. He lives in Brooklyn and is the editor of *Cello Entry*, a poetry journal.

PIOTR UKLANSKI is a Polish artist. His book, *The Nazis*, will be published in June, 1999.

ALISSA WALSER was born in 1961. She studied painting in New York and Vienna and lives in Frankfurt am Main. "Given" was awarded the Ingeborg Bachmann Prize and is the first of ten linked stories in her collection, *This Is Not My Entire Story* (*Dies ist nich meine ganze Geschichte*), published in German by Rowolt in 1994.

M.E. YANKELEVICH is currently working on translations of Daniil Kharms's and Alexander Vvedensky's writing. His fiction has been anthologized in *Voices from the Heartland.* He lives in Brooklyn.

AMINE ZAITZEFF lives in Westchester, New York. These are her first published stories.

26 lectures

exhibition

SoundLab performance

Five29Ninety9

a one-day symposium

Wandering through the urban structure of New York City, participating in different fields of production, meeting people, and exchanging thoughts and information, one circulates in an endless flow of heterogeneous cultural knowledge. Institutions assume a role of systematizing this flow. Motivated by specific agendas and interests, the discourse of institutions is necessarily constituted from within. Outside and between the wide range of institutions, individuals build temporal spaces of flexible exchange which emerge, disappear, and reform. Five29Ninety9 recognizes this fluid, social process as a resource in itself. The aim of the symposium is to create a surface rather than a container, a quorum with no prescribed conclusion. Five29Ninety9 is for people interested in contemporary/political/intellectual discussions in the context of cultural production. The exhibition offers all participants—the speakers as well as the audience—space and a VCR/monitor to show artwork. The exhibition will continually change, reflecting the audience as it comes and goes. Speakers, audience, and exhibitors are asked to describe, define, and take responsibility for the present moment.

speakers include:

Beth Coleman, Martin Conrads, Dyke Action Machine (DAM!), Yolande Daniels, Katja Eydel, Ciara Finnegan, Leah Gilliam, Howard Goldkrand, Brian Hand, Lana Lin, May Day Productions, Tim Maul/Fred Szynanski, Sally McKay, Nils Norman, Walid Raad, Orla Ryan, Reginald Cortez Woolery, Florian Wüst

at St. Ann's Church Saturday May 29th 9am-1am

157 Montague St. at the corner of Clinton St.
located in Brooklyn Heights, N/R train to Court St. (1st stop in Brooklyn)

NICOLE CARSTENS
MARY ESCH
JOHN HANSEL
ALEXEI HAY
ENOC PEREZ
EVE SUSSMAN
GORDON TERRY

BIANCA
www.artnewyork.com

Bronwyn Keenan

3 CROSBY STREET NEW YORK NY 10013 T212 431 5083 F212 431 3327 EMAIL bkg@artnewyork.com

STEFFANY MARTZ

529 West 20th Street 6th floor New York, NY 10011
t:212.206.3686 f:212.206.3654

ISSUE #4

Stories by Cyril Connolly, Thomas McGuane, Jim Thompson, Samantha Gillison, Michael Brownstein, Emily Carter. Art by Julianne Swartz and Peter Nadin. Poems by David Berman and Nick Tosches. Plus Denis Johnson in Somalia. (A monster issue, sales undercut by slightly rash choice of cover art by editors. Get it while you can! $15)

ISSUE #5

Stories by David Foster Wallace, Siobhan Reagan, Irvine Welsh. Jerome Badanes's brilliant novella, *Change or Die*. Poems by David Berman and Vito Acconci. Plus Helen Thorpe on the murder of Ireland's most famous female journalist, and Delmore Schwartz on T. S. Eliot's squint. (A must-have at only $15!)

ISSUE #6

Stories by James Purdy, Strawberry Saroyan, and Michael Cunningham. Poems by Rick Moody, Deborah Garrison, Monica Lewinsky, Charlie Smith. Art by Matthew Ritchie, Ellen Harvey, Cindy Stefans. Rem Koolhaas Project. With a beautiful cover by Adam Fuss. (Unclutter our offices by requesting this blockbuster for only $10.)

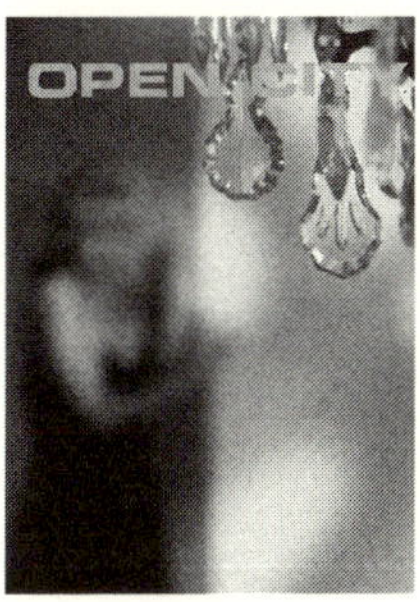

ISSUE #7

Stories by Mary Gaitskill, Bliss Broyard, and Sam Lipsyte. Poems by David Berman, Elizabeth Macklin, Steve Malkmus, and Will Oldham. Art by Jimmy Raskin, Laura Larson, and Jeff Burton. (We've cheapened ourselves with our new quarterly schedule, so don't get caught with gaps in your collection! $10)

Please send a check or money order payable to *The Segue Foundation*. Don't forget to specify the issue number and give us your address. Send checks to:

OPEN CITY 225 Lafayette Street, Suite 1114, New York, NY 10012

"Some day, I think, he will inspire a crucifixion."
(Leebron, page 111)

Where I Am Now

Harvey Shapiro

I seem to be withdrawing from my life slowly
like pulling out from an alcoholic fuck.
Savoring it but glad that it's over. Tired
and not knowing what to do next.

History

Harvey Shapiro

I have lived three-quarters of a century.
I remember the man bringing ice
into the kitchen for the icebox.
He came down the narrow alley
that led to the back of the house.
He used tongs to lift the ice.
Our first car was a Nash.
From our window on Riverside Drive
I saw them building the George Washington Bridge.
When you had ice cream at home
your mother had to make it.
Cases of Dr. Brown's Celray Tonic and Cream Soda.
I kissed my cousin Muriel under the piano.

How Charley Shaver Died

Harvey Shapiro

He had a gig
but he was hurting.
His doctor said, play the date,
then check into the hospital.
That night, when the party ended
and the band packed up,
Charley started to give stuff away—
his watch, his rings—to the women
in the room. Then
he circled the room with his horn,
playing: "For all I know we may never meet again."
At this point, the man who was telling the story
in the locker room at the Manhattan Plaza gym
and who had sung the line slowly, with
a pause between each word, began to cry.

"I'm looking for another building to move to, or another city."
(Wenclas, page 199)

Girl Games

Caitlin O'Connor Creevy

I HAVE AN AMPLE RUMP AND LARGE BREASTS, AND MY HAIR IS RED and long and wavy. I am a sexy girl. My face is a pretty Irish face; when it is made up, it becomes beautiful to strangers—my green eyes, when delicately lined with black, and gently smudged with gray, have been called "smoldering"; my cheekbones, brushed with the slightest wisp of blush—"defined"; my lips, when coated with a soft mauve, and perhaps, at night, an almost imperceptible cherry glaze, are indefatigably "kissable." Sometimes, after I prepare my face, I must stay with the mirror for a little while longer, because I look so hot I want to touch my boobs and do it with myself.

When I was six, living in a small house in the suburbs of Chicago, I locked my bedroom door, took all my clothes off, and pretended I was posing for *Oui* magazine. I lay on my side propped up by one arm, facing the make-believe camera, closed my eyes, and arched my back. Then I lay down on my bed (the "camera" would be above me) and spread my legs—very slowly, just the action of spreading them was rushing me, making my six-year-old vagina swell. Then I would matter-of-factly open my small, innocent vagina with my fingers, so that the "camera" could get a close-up.

After my imagination sensed the satisfaction of the invisible photographer, my mind raced ahead to a vision of a forest. I was walking alone, dark shadows making scary shapes all around, when a strong man came out of the trees and slammed me to the ground. He pinned me while I kicked, covered my mouth while

I screamed, and pressed my chest to the ground. He brushed his cheek against my shoulders. His hands were big. His face was very handsome, and his muscles were strange. He touched my hair as if he were a curious animal. I was becoming excited, but I snapped out of it and tried to escape. I wrangled as hard as I could from beneath his massive body, but, ultimately, he overpowered me. At that point, I put my tiny finger inside my vagina and almost fell off the bed.

Nobody ever tried to rape me. I didn't have weird uncles or a weird dad or stepdad or plumber or violin teacher. I was a nymph developing my sexuality, and I had just seen a pornographic magazine. Pornography had never been in our house before; someone had probably given it to my dad as a gag gift, and he held on to it for a while, in spite of himself. Maybe he actually bought it, for chrissake, I don't know. But who cares. I was six and saw a porno. I don't believe my reaction was cause for psychological alarm. I was a dramatic child.

More than anything else in the world, I wanted to be pregnant. At that time, I didn't understand that I had about 400,000 eggs in my ovaries, and that I needed one to ripen, ripen like a mischievous drupe. I needed cells to multiply around my egg to form a follicle. Then for that follicle-wollicle to push its way to the surface of the ovary-bovary. Burst. And release the egg. Poof. Ovulation. Then off to the Fallopian. I needed just one sperm out of a jerk-off's 300,000,000—just one to enter my special place, wriggle through the uterus, into the F-tube. Bang. Fertilization. I didn't know that that was what I wanted. I simply always wanted to be pregnant.

Early on, I took steps towards realizing my goal. At age eight I founded the S.E.X. club. My best friends were my cousins Millie and Bridgette, and I roped them into membership. I was poor and they were rich, but I was oldest and that was the only thing that mattered then. We stole a dusty bottle of rum from the bar in the basement of my grandparents' mansion and sneaked it to the bushes for our inaugural meeting. The rules were:

1) Take a swig of rum.

We passed the bottle between us, none of us having any idea how much it would kill our virgin tongues and throats. But the nubile triumvirate survived the upsetting swig and I soon announced the next phase of S.E.X. hazing.

2) Swear.

This eliminated Millie. She refused.

"Bitch," said Bridgette.

"Asshole," I said.

It was a pretty July day in "Chicagoland," as they say on the radio, maybe even a little too warm; and as Millie dug a hole with a stick and Bridgette looked skeptical, I announced the final test.

3) Run around the yard (landscaped in the Naturalist style) surrounding my grandparents' house, number fourteen, the grandest lot on a very private drive that was regularly trafficked by service vans of a great variety of service providers—duct cleaners, personal car washers, drapery launderers—anything that extracted dirt for money; and observed by discriminating neighbors walking "Barky," their emotional sponge; and, perhaps most threatening of all, tromped daily by Aunt Snowy, who would soon come out to suntan with a Tab on ice.

Run around the yard—naked.

This eliminated Bridgette. I stripped as B & M became increasingly nervous and giggly. Then I took my thrilling jog—proud and scared—around number fourteen. Only the teenage daughter from number eight drove by, and at that point I was a hair's breadth away from the waterfall, barely visible from the road; I didn't even see the bouncy neighbor pass, but I could hear Millie scream, and was informed about it after I came around the bend, breathless, at that point having experienced dread, power, and orgasm.

I fell into the bushes, my safety. The bushes formed a walled fortress around the property, about six feet high, and inside them was our little forest.

"Oh my God. Oh my God. Jeannie, Jeannie, that girl Jeannie drove by," Millie sputtered.

"I cannot believe you just did that, you are so queer," Bridgette went on, half-laughing, shocked.

"Cover me up! Cover me up!" I said, and the two of them, eight and seven, huddled over me like Chinese wise men. After I had dressed, we loped around the bushes assessing the damage. Did we get away with it?

Yes.

Oh, like all kids, we played fishy games—like the spanking game, where Millie pretended she was the mom and I was the bad girl, in which she spanked my bare bottom until it was burning red, then put toothpaste on as a salve. But all in all, childhood was a happy time.

As I got older, I didn't see Bridgette and Millie as much; they were at Ford and I was at Locke, both posh private schools in the city. Ironically, I, the broke kid of the broken branch of the family, was going to the even snobbier school, tuition bills being paid by my dead grandparents, guiding the course of my life from beneath the grass. I couldn't complain. No, I could not complain.

Things in high school weren't as bad as they could have been, although it was strange being the only one in my class who experienced house-shame and difficult assembling deceptive costumes day after day. I did have my best friend, Ann, though, the perfect partner in crime—shockingly beautiful, just shy of six feet, Ann was something of a stoner, but as a Communist puppeteer, she had a duty to get high. Ann has always struggled with the fact that with the development of a slight eating disorder and a smidge of discipline, she could have had a successful modeling career.

Ann and I met our freshman year. We both smoked. After a few rendezvous on the stairs, she started talking. I thought she was a big liar. She told me she was having a relationship with her friend's dad. She said he "looked at her" and she "looked at him." I don't know, maybe it was true. At that point I thought she was weird. Weird for screwing around with people's dads or weird for lying. Our first time alone in the world together, we went to the corner store to get some salt-and-sour potato chips, and when we walked out, she gave me ten candies—Jolly Ranchers, mini Reese's, etc. She had stolen them—which I thought was incredible. I had a hard time with shoplifting. So I didn't like Ann at first. I didn't believe in her, and I thought she was trying to be cool.

The thing was that she *was* cool. She was a bitchy genius and a stone-cold fox. Her hair was jet black and her blue eyes could ice lakes of fire. She looked like a weird Saharan princess who was exquisitely graceful, especially while killing. Ann was going out with Frick, a junior, who had already totaled three BMWs. Ann could deal with that scene; she was schooled. Her dad was a hippie from Florida who made huge cash in self-help. After taking off with the baby-sitter (he was creative), Mills kept up a decent bank account for Ann, a most amorphous fund that would sometimes vanish, then magically reappear. The ATM was always a bit of a crap shoot. Her mom was a tiny blonde beauty queen who had literally fallen to fucking pieces after her husband took off. Ann was never as stoned as her mom.

My mom, on the other hand, was never stoned. And why would she be? Jeez, I was hard on my mom, as if I wanted her to be stoned. Stoned moms are not so enviable. I wanted to be-pregnant-be-pregnant-be-pregnant, i.e., be a mother. Meanwhile I despised my own mother. Was pregnancy some sort of a contest? That I could succeed where she failed? That I could be loving and real, instead of emotionally shrewd and deceptive? Or maybe I wanted to pass the baton, put myself in charge, believing I could become an authority, physically, by having a belly filled with my own child. Maybe I could diminish her power over me by reaching the same level she had; or understand what her power over me was, and break it.

I could never figure out why my dad married her. Dad was cool. He was funny, the Life of the Party. In eighth grade, he came and took me out of school to go to the Museum of Science and Industry (my brother was too young), and we stared at the geodesic dome on permanent display while he explained that geodesic domes have proved to be the strongest structures ever devised, that earthquakes cannot damage them, that they shelter Arctic radar, and that the best ones are proportionally thinner than a chicken-egg shell is to the egg. He knew what was going on in the world; he read six papers a day. Granted, it was because he was unemployed most of the time, but he maximized his leisure.

I could never spend time the way he did. I spent a lot of time worrying that time was slipping through my fingers. I spent nights staring, wondering how I was going to do the innumerable things

I needed to do. It wasn't until I was eighteen that I discovered genuine leisure, not coincidentally when I left home. Freshman year at Columbia was about naps, imported beer, "getting to know" homeless people, drinking Turkish coffee and pretending to like it, et cetera. I returned to the heartland "New Yorked," with a string of intolerable affectations and a distinctly collegiate change in my sensibility about intoxicants and my own sophistication.

Winter break after our first semester at college, Ann and I spent every second together. Ann cooked up numerous schemes, including a very late night in Cicero, a faraway suburb that is deeply Chicagoan and rumored to stay open until 6 A.M. As we shared a $1.99 plate of eggs and link sausage at a booth in one of Cicero's greasier spoons, we reflected upon our brush with death.

"Could you pass the ketchup?" Ann said, pointing at a bottle on the table to my right. I reached over and grabbed the ketchup, taking the opportunity to smile at a police officer sitting at the booth behind us. Being flanked by cops, ironically, was exactly where we wanted to be, as we were trying not to have another run-in with Jerry, the used car salesman who "liked to party" and with whom we had spent the past hour doing drugs. We had run out on Jerry when he went into his bedroom to grab another bag. It was a mad dash down the Cicero streets, and we were breathless and wild eyed when we arrived at the Dodge. But we figured that if we could just sit tight for a while, after a few hundred cigarettes and two dollars worth of chow, we would have the gusto to make it the necessary blocks to our lost car in the sub-zero early morning.

"Do you remember the name of that street?" I questioned Ann seriously.

"God, no," Ann said, wrapping the last bit of toast around her sausage and stuffing it into her mouth.

"No...wait, is it Chaswick? Or Cheswick or something? Some sort of Arkansas subdivision name, like Pembley Arms or something like that."

"Starkey," I blurted.

Desire, our waitress, shuffled over in a housecoat and placed our check under the sugar, then shuffled back out. I could hear the back door swing open and shut, and through the windows I could see her going to sleep on a cot next door.

"Starkey, exactly," Ann said as she patted her napkin to the corners of her lips with her left hand and searched with her right hand for the pack of cigarettes she kept swearing she had put in her jacket pocket.

The table of cops that were in front of us got up to leave.

"Thank God," mumbled Ann.

It was good to be rid of that set of cops; they were beginning to look a little suspicious. The other table of cops behind us was more than enough to ward off Jerry, and furthermore I was developing a crush on the officer I smiled at while smuggling the ketchup. For the sake of vanity, I tried not to scratch my itching head violently—a real sacrifice.

"I can't find my cigarettes," Ann said after she had shuffled through her purse and coat for the fifth or sixth time. Just at that moment the remaining table of four cops got up to leave. I felt a pang of fear and urgency. Two of the four policemen put dollars on the table and left, leaving the cute one and his partner to take care of the final exchange at the cash register. The cute one was eyeing me, clearly stalling as his partner made the moves to go; and when they went to the counter to pay, I caught a glimpse of his badge. On the way out the door, Officer Chris Proscinski fumbled for a cigarette. He stopped to light it and was embarrassed to ask me if I wanted one, although he knew my predicament; it was impossible not to have overheard Ann and me as we lamented our lost Camels. I picked up my cue.

"You don't happen to have an extra smoke, do you?" I asked.

"Sure," said Officer Proscinski, and he handed me a freshly packed cigarette, and then another, as an afterthought. Naturally, he wanted to make sure Ann was taken care of, too.

"Do you know where Starkey Street is?" I asked.

"Starkey Street?"

"I think that's the name of it. Starkey or Starkley or something," I said.

"John, you don't know where Starkey Street is, do you?" Officer Proscinski asked his partner.

The other officer shook his head no, then approached our

table in a coppish way.

"What's the problem here, girls?" he said with a scary voice.

"We can't find our car. We don't exactly know what street it's on," Ann said as if she were talking to her stepmother, Buni (pronounced "bunny"), a person she considered her inferior and enemy.

"That is a problem," grumbled the policeman, tilting his head in such a way that his excess neck was forced to bubble over the stiff, starched collar of his uniform. His badge, identifying him as John Zurcher, gleamed in the fluorescence.

The men in blue said that we could come with them, that they would help us find our car. After about an hour of driving around we finally stumbled upon my gold Chrysler LeBaron, nicknamed "The Fiddler" because of a bumper sticker that read "I Fiddled Around at Fiddlesticks" that had been left on the car by its former owner, a sap named Don Kerman who sold a bag factory to my uncle. Ann and I jumped out of the warm 5-0 into our own sweet ride. Officer Proscinski swiftly appeared at the driver's window.

I rolled the window down.

"Thanks so much," I cooed.

"No problem," said Chris.

Chris stood there for a moment.

"Do you want to come in and have a cigarette?" I asked. I could afford to offer, since the group, on our crusade to find the car, had stopped at a 7-Eleven and Chris had bought me a pack.

"Sure," said Chris, and he hopped in the back seat, a little too eagerly. I was slightly grossed out by him because of the couple of unfunny things he said as we drove around, but I was still able to round up some desire for this pig. After we smoked, he began to massage my shoulders by digging his thumbs and forefingers into my tendons so hard I lost my vision. Ann was trying to fake sleep in the front seat, but it became obvious fast that a new arrangement had to be made. Ann got out of the car saying that she had left her gloves somewhere. Once we were alone, Chris promptly got up front and began to maul me.

This grossed me out definitely, and I decided to suck him off and end the thing as quickly as possible.

His professional pants made me edgy, but they came down just like any other. His gun and billy club surrounded me like headphones, and I pretended to hear nothing.

"You better make me come, you dead little baby," he said as I licked his balls. Then he thrust his pelvis and jabbed his dick in my mouth, grunting, "Make. . .Me. . .Come. . ."

As I slid that fucker's spindly dick in and out of my mouth, I had to hold back the vomit. I so desperately wanted it to be over. The little ridges on his penis slid against my tongue as I tried so hard to make him come. I sucked and rammed his cock against the back of my throat. Don't puke, I thought, just a few more seconds, I know he's ready to blast. My need to be successful pushed me to hold out and bob my head faster and faster. For one second I reveled in the humiliation. I felt like a nothing, just a body to be used for this man to get off. I felt like a little worthless slut, and, for one weird dark minute, I liked it.

After I swallowed his bitter load and gagged three times, I sat up and pulled myself together. I whispered, "I'd better rescue Ann."

Chris zipped his fly and followed me, looking from side to side. Ann was asleep in the backseat of the cop car and Zurcher was talking on the CB. I tapped on the glass and Zurcher ignored me, infusing massive doses of condescension into his feigned obliviousness. Ann woke up and hobbled back to my car.

I turned the key and the car commented that "the door is ajar," in its grating, electronic way. The Fiddler is one of the "talking cars" Chrysler manufactured in the 1980s, a model they have since taken off the market.

Twenty minutes into the drive home, Ann broke the silence, "You didn't fuck him, did you?"

"No," I answered.

"Good."

"Why do you ask?"

"The fat cop said he's HIV. You're fine, though."

"Well, what the fuck are you saying to me? Why didn't you come and break in the doors and get me the fuck away from him!"

"Because that fat-ass just grumbled it to me as you were coming to get me out of the goddamn cop car, after I'd been shoved out of our car going *home*, after you were screwing some turd, that's why!"

I didn't know what to say.

"You need to go back to rehab, Annie. You're really showing."

I drove Ann to her mom's apartment and continued on to my own family's home in the suburbs.

As I eased around the bend back onto Lake Shore Drive, I thought about Chris Proscinski's prick, skinny and hard; I could tell what it looked like even before I saw it. It poked me when he rubbed against my legs. That poking prick was one of the incentives for me to opt for a blow job. I sure as hell didn't want to have sex with this guy. But why didn't I say, "Get out of the fucking car now"? Or even "Um, could you please get out of the car now?" Maybe because I was scared he would beg me in a mean way, maybe I felt like he really wanted to get some come out and I was supposed to help him do it. But why was I supposed to help him do it? Why did I feel obligated? I was lazy, yes, I didn't want to hassle with the whiny pleas he would inevitably lay on me, but I felt bad, too. I felt bad for him. He wanted it. I had gotten him hot, I guess. I'd flirted relentlessly. But, God, I didn't want to touch him. Sex stopped being about pregnancy or seeds or any other crap. I didn't want to touch his skin, even by accident.

I was good at being a tease. I found success in it. I could turn guys on—dumb guys who liked sex, yeah, I could turn them on. I could stick out my D-tits, tilt my head and act thirteen. I gave them fake innocence. But then I felt like I had to deliver, and that's when I graduated from a tease to a slut.

The problem now was that this guy had AIDS and called me a "dead little baby." Chances were slim that I had been infected by him, but I had touched the disease and could feel it coming. I curled into a ball every night, convincing myself that I would be punished for all my carelessness and self-disrespect. I tossed and turned, hopelessly trapped in my own skin; I covered my face under the covers and cried, wondering what the fuck I was doing.

Ann's analysis of my promiscuity was that I wanted to screw my dad. I think Ann really did want to screw her dad because she was obsessed with the idea of girls screwing their dads. And what, I wanted to screw my dad more than anyone else? Jesus, I couldn't touch my dad's underwear that were in the laundry room—where they had been fastidiously washed, bleached, and folded by my mother, if not starched and pressed lying there on top of his pile like threadbare pillows for wayward midget hobos—much less envision what went into them. Gross. Ann's proposal unnerved me, of course, and I kept worrying that I was inappropriately repulsed at the thought of doing it with my father.

"I really can't buy that, Ann."

"It's so fucking simple. You hate your mom because you want your dad to love you. He doesn't give you that much attention. You're desperate. You have sex with anyone to replace your dad. On a deeper level, you want to make love with your dad: ultimate proof."

"But he does give me attention."

"No, he used to give you attention. He, like, took you to a museum when you were eight and you're still gaga over it. That was a decade ago. I don't know. Maybe I'm too harsh. My dad's just such an ass, maybe I think all dads are asses. No, your dad is cool."

"I mentioned that thing with the museum, I think once maybe twice, because we were talking about domes. 'Gaga' over my dad taking me to a museum? That's a little . . ." I trailed off, eating another baby carrot from the bag on the kitchen counter.

"The mention of the Astrodome wouldn't really jog my memory about some fucking day trip ten years ago with a man who had nothing better to do, unless I was slightly obsessed."

"Okay, you're a bitch," I said.

Ann stood there staring, then went to the refrigerator and fixed a little dipping bowl of ranch dressing.

"I'm sorry," she said, putting the bowl on the table in front of me.

Then the weirdest thing happened. Tears started falling out of her eyes. She seemed a little shocked by them. I didn't know what to do. God knows she wouldn't want me to hold her.

"Do you want some Kleenex?. . .or. . .some toilet paper? I don't think we have any Kleenex," I said.

"No, no," she said, wiping the stuff away with her hands.

I offered her some of the ranch dip, but she shook her head, and I tried to put the bowl back on the counter discreetly.

"Buni had a baby," she said.

Oh, God, I thought, Her dad really is an ass. How did she find out about this—did he actually call? I had never met Mr. Miller, but I remember the one time he called—from the airport. He called Ann to say that he was in Chicago, but that it was a short stop. He was sorry, he wouldn't be able to see her, but he would be back again some other time. That set her and her mom back about six months. What would this news do?

It was odd. Ann acted like such a little kid about her father—like a ten-year-old whose parents had just divorced. I blithely believed that people our age with faraway dads really were "over it," as they claimed to be. But maybe because her parents split when she was thirteen, at the brink of her sexuality, and maybe because her absentee father was her lifeline, she was not.

"I have a little brother now, isn't that stupid? Isn't it stupid? I don't know her. I don't know him. Fuck. Who cares. Who knows anyone," she said, in a hopeless voice I'd never heard her use before.

Buni had a baby. My God, that was impossible to stomach. Buni, at that point, was sixteen—two years younger than we were. It's no mystery that Ann had complexes; not to mention that she would be eighteen in a month, and Daddy just got a brand new kid. The clock was ticking. Ann had always feared being cut off without a word, but now it was a very real possibility.

Ann gave off a distinct "don't touch me" vibe; her physical self needed nothing, it's true, but she was a tender heart—sometimes, I thought, pathologically so. She was a mad gift giver, giving the most thoughtful presents to anyone with whom she had even the vaguest relationship, and showering those she did know. My mom had a shelf exclusively filled with gifts from Ann. She gave my great-aunt Betsy an antique lemonade pitcher and a matching set of etched glass tumblers for summertime, her driver's-ed teacher a book about Delorean, her boyfriend's best friend's girlfriend a ceramic box shaped like a violin, because the girl mentioned that she had played in high school and wanted to take it up again. The worrisome thing, though, was the homemade candies, her favorite thing to distribute. Ann would slave in the kitchen with paraffin wax and gum paste, pulling taffy or taking the temperature of her nougat to see if it was at the "softball stage"; she could make Newport creams, divinity, rock candy, for God's sake; she knew her way around a penuche and she was working on Hawaiian centers. If she dropped ten pounds, she could make $10,000 a day. She was skinny as it was, but she had to become emaciated to be a professional, and she did not have the discipline. But there was another side to her resistance to modeling—a great part of her soul wanted to be one of "the people," which to her meant nothing less than being an impoverished Cuban.

Her fundamental belief was that life was not fair, but that it should be. That everyone had rights to an innumerable list of things: a doctor's care when dying, running water, not getting shot on the way to school, and so on. Like many nineties leftists she had a great reverence and love for all things Hispanic, à la Che Guevara, and always said "Gracias" (*con acento*) whenever we encountered a Mexican person at a checkout counter; this never failed to embarrass me—it seemed like imposed camaraderie to me. But Ann felt that the fight was on and that the people needed help and organization to make things happen, so she did things like construct a fifty-foot papier-mâché gas pump and drag it in front of the White House to protest the World Bank. She had an unbelievable romance with poverty and agricultural society. Her annual escape to a Marxist puppet farm in Vermont included helping with chores, like gathering wood or pumping water from the well; sleeping on the cold, wet ground protected by nothing but a scratchy wool blanket, and eating basic peasant meals made from the food of the land. To Ann, that was glory—although she could never get enough filet mignon, invariably enjoying the latter with a side of postconsumption anti-rich commentary ("fat preppies, the kill, etc."). Maybe her constant struggle with drug addiction was a way to create a happy medium between the world of total glamour and the revolution.

Sometimes it queered me out to think about the pain behind the Most Popular Girl's pretty face. It wasn't as though I was Ann's bookworm sidekick who secretly wanted to kiss her. I loved her, but our friendship wasn't a case of one idolizing the other, at least not that I could see. Politically, we were polar opposites.

I wanted to follow in the footsteps of Zsa Zsa Gabor. I spent my nineteenth summer in Gabor's native Hungary, where I could never get enough filet mignon—literally. I came away from every fine dining experience with that much more desperation to be swank. I read *Tess* on the banks of the Danube, then cried on a train all the way to Italy. My European stint only encouraged my reproduction obsession. I saw first-rate genes everywhere I looked on that continent. I wanted to establish a chain of cloning kiosks in every town square. On my plane ride back to the USA, I decided to focus on bioethics within my pre-med degree.

Back in New York, school was hardish. I spent Monday through Friday, 5 P.M. to 9 P.M. at the library. My library time evaporated quickly. My brain cooked systematically, following instructions, until my watch beeped, then I could return to my human persona. I did take a five-minute break on each hour, which I spent doodling. As a kid, I had read the Sex section of our old encyclopedia a thousand times. I could never forget the bit about fertilization being introduced into the mammalian body artificially, "with a pipette." Pipette. What an ill plan B. But I considered it. I thought maybe if I could hose the sperm directly into the Fallopian tube using some sort of glass-rod blower . . .

Enough, I would note mentally. I would return to my studies, settling deeper into my cubby and plowing ahead until my watch beeped at 8:55. (I needed five minutes to put my books into my backpack, return materials, take a drink at the water fountain, and so on.)

At nine o'clock, after library time, I would run out into the streets, famished. I might think about going for Indian, but I would end up going to the pizzeria instead, in hopes that the Johnny was there, a loaded pistol of virility who was probably twelve; the Johnny was straight out of Sicily, so he had been having sex for years. I usually ordered a simple cheese slice, and when I did, the Johnny would murmur, "Hot?" I would stare at him as if I didn't understand the question. He would blush, open and close his eyes, which caused a small breeze, pivot to the oven and back, then gently slide the burning triangle onto the paper moon that he placed in my sweaty palms. If he could just jizz on the damn thing, maybe that would expedite things. The Johnny's scorching sperm would be a sure hit; I should move into action phase with him.

At about three o'clock in the morning, I would sleep, and dream again about being pregnant. Dream of a living heart, smaller than an apple seed, beating inside of me. New blood pulsing. Wrists forming to make a place for hands. A brain and spine developing, connecting. Eyelids growing, too young to open. Transparent skin holding together the small body that was twisting and turning with fresh life, kicking against my ribs, and listening to my voice. I would dream of my own skin changing colors, my body changing shape, and my temperature rising. Of everything coming together inside, then my little baby floating out of me into two unknown people's arms. Before I woke up, I would dream that a tree wrapped around me, and the leaves whispered in my ears that I was forgiven.

After graduation, I landed back in Chicago at my parents' house, prepared to "move on." I had been there for about a month; things were okay. I was pretty much just going out with Ann and developing a crop of brain-damaged complexes about my identity and future. Ann finally interrogated me about my longing for pregnancy. "What is your problem?" she asked. She had had her first abortion at fifteen, "snuffed the life out," and could not understand why I wanted to give my freedom away. My mom was bugging me with her attempts to befriend me, and I was bugged at myself for being bugged. There was no reason I shouldn't be kind to my mother; she was a mild-mannered, organized woman who had always been kind to me, not to mention the fact that she created me. But why is it that mild manners suggest a body full of excruciating hate and rage, and organization seems like a symptom of this disease? Mom tried to forge our relationship in her own way. As part of her current friendship plan, she made an appointment for the two of us for a "day of beauty" at a second-rate local salon. I am always up for a manicure, but I didn't want to tell her that I didn't want a facial at this place. There are a number of beauty machines that use electroshock, and it is unwise to undergo questionable versions of such treatments. I didn't want to jump to conclusions, though. Maybe they had a more organic program at Curl Up 'N Dye.

The day arrived, remarkably close to the end of a night, the only trace of which I recall was Ann banging on my next door neighbor's window and demanding breakfast burritos. That was around six, and I was scheduled for a nine o'clock facial with Pam. I wasn't in the mood for a facial. In fact, a blood transfusion would have been much more refreshing. Should I have warned Pam not to touch me? Inform her that the clouds of gin fumes rising from my flesh were not a definite problem but that the pound of marijuana presently rewiring my system was making me a bit sensitive? If she could just concentrate on my eyeballs—just pour some sort of antifreeze, or the exact opposite, or fucking *something* on them, that would be great.

As soon as her hands touched my cheek, I knew I had to get out of there. I put my shirt back on and went into the next room where Mom was getting a makeover. I listened as the makeup artist described the "trendy look" and, through my own pained eyes, watched the misguided application of purple shadow on my mom's haggard lids.

"Mom."

"Hmm."

"I think I have hemorrhoids." Shit, I meant to say cramps but I said hemorrhoids instead. Maybe I did have hemorrhoids.

She looked up at me and surveyed my general appearance: slovenly, green.

"Get out of here," she said.

Ouch. I really was an asshole. Oh, well, I would deal with that problem later. How was I going to get back into bed? I could take a cab, but I had no cash. I guessed I could run into my house, find cash.

My cab ride home was a dream. The cab pulled up in front of my house and I told the driver to hold on. The front door was open, which was odd but not that odd; sometimes it doesn't close all the way. (Maintenance was sort of a non-issue at our pad.) I thought maybe I could find some cash in the front room, but that was not realistic. I was looking, like, in the remote control holder. Ann wasn't on the couch. She must have crawled out the door and gotten a cab—in the A.M. Bravo! I thought, and started walking toward my room when I heard strange sounds. The TV was on, maybe it was the TV.

I stopped midway through the hall. I couldn't decide if I wanted to see and make sure or if I didn't need to make sure. That sick old bed was creaking, Dad was moaning, and Ann was grunting, "I'm coming, Daddy. . .I'm coming." I stood frozen on the brown shag, the ugly, battered path between the front room and the backrooms. Then I heard the sound of a hand against skin, followed by Ann's muffled "ugh." A spank, I realized. My dad was fucking and spanking Ann in the bed where I was conceived.

The cabbie laid on the horn.

I walked softly back down the hall into the front room, where I saw Ann's things scattered around. I grabbed her black leather bag and ran back out to the cab and jumped inside.

"What you going to do?" the driver barked.

"Cash machine," I muttered. "Go to 7-Eleven. Go to the cash machine."

"No one knew who bought the eyes."
(Police Blotter, page 107)

Westchester Burning

Amine Zaitzeff

1. You Can Be Sure

IN 1984 PHILLIP AND I BOUGHT A HOUSE IN BEDFORD AS AN investment. We planned to rent the house out. The money we received in rent would almost pay for the mortgage, and the appreciation on the house would, through the years, pay for our children's college education.

We bought the house from Mrs. Keenan. Her husband had owned a chain of taverns in the Bronx, Erin Forever. He died of a heart attack the day they moved in, leaving her alone to raise their six sons. Her youngest was going to Michigan University on an athletic scholarship and she didn't need a large house anymore.

We had the eleven rooms painted Navajo White, the downstairs floors refinished, and the upstairs recarpeted in a medium pile, light green. We rented the house to a divorced orthopedic surgeon and his two grown sons. After six months they stopped paying rent. The doctor quit his practice and became a bodybuilder. His sons held part time jobs as landscapers.

"It's not easy evicting tenants," a litigation partner told Phillip.

Four months later they were gone.

They took their forty sets of bodybuilding equipment and opened "Bodies by George" in Hartsdale. The business was registered in the doctor's mother's name. They left five dogs, two of them dead, eight cats, and two ferrets.

Phillip took a day off from work, got the animals in cages, and brought them to the local ASPCA. The Department of Public Works removed the dogs that had died.

The house was fumigated and the real-estate agent advised us to renovate the house before putting it on the market.

"You have a great investment here. Money you spend on it, you'll double. It's in a great location, great family neighborhood, and the house is on five acres. Yes, the land in the back slopes down suddenly, but that's not a problem. Five acres is still five acres. Bedford zoning law allows one horse per acre. You can have five horses here."

Phillip told me the house was now my baby, but he would still have to approve all expenditures.

There were three estimates for the work; Phillip went with the middle bid.

"Mrs. Calt," said the contractor, "you can't get these urine stains out. No amount of sanding will do it. The whole downstairs. Upstairs? It went right through the carpeting. All the floors. In every room. You'll have to retile the bathrooms, it went right through the grout. It's a good thing that the floor in the basement is cement. Cement is pretty indestructible. All we need to do with that is wash it down with a strong chemical solution and then paint it. A nice battleship gray.

"Mrs. Calt, since your husband okayed replacing the floor, why don't you suggest knocking out the wall between the kitchen and family room to him? There's a big hole in it anyway. This way you'll get to see a nice fire burning in the fireplace as you're making dinner."

The contractor hired a subcontractor for the kitchen counters and cabinets. The contractor was paid, but instead of paying the subcontractor, he became ill and moved to Florida, where bankruptcy laws are lenient.

Phillip hired the contractor who had come in with the highest bid.

"Mrs. Calt, did you know that they laid the new flooring over rotted subflooring? There's no way you can save what was put down. Everything will have to be ripped up. If you like, we'll cut it up for you and you can use it for kindling. We'll give you a new subflooring and we'll use wood that's been kiln dried. This way it won't buckle up at you. We'll lay down brand-new oak floors and you can be sure the job will be done right this time."

The house didn't sell. It was a problem that most of the five acres were unusable. It was advised to landfill the gully, remove the weeping willows, and create an expansive lawn. I saw the two sons of the doctor on the landscaping crew. One was operating the bulldozer and the other one was driving the truck with the rocks.

It took about a year after the Wall Street crash of 1987 for the bottom to fall out of the real-estate market. It was then that Phillip told me I had ruined his life.

Why do I believe, at age fifty-two, that by spraying Yves Saint Laurent's Rive Gauche near the open window of my attic bedroom, it will replace the smell of my first cigarette of the morning? That the strong, sweet, scent will be enough to mask what I have done? What can he say? Can he hurt me more?

He came home last night after I finally fell asleep. He did come home, because when I came downstairs his door was closed, shut tight by the black sock he uses as a doorjamb.

During the renovation of the house, the doorknobs from all the doors were removed. The doors were stripped of old paint, planed, sanded, primed, and repainted. The doorknobs were placed in two large plastic buckets.

"Mrs. Calt, we can't find the doorknobs. Someone must have taken them or else they were thrown out by mistake. They're gone. I don't even know where to tell you to get them. They're an odd size. They'd have to be specially made up. It'll be expensive, since they were solid brass and old."

Phillip now uses one of his black socks to hold his door shut. The door that opens to the room that was once ours and is now his. He sleeps alone.

He'll have someone. He takes care of himself. Cycling on weekends, using lite mayonnaise, having one brimming glass of red wine to help clear his arteries and to be safe, a small piece of Belgian chocolate. He uses firming neck cream. He takes vitamins E, A, C (1000 mg.), and B complex, zinc, calcium, folic acid, and selenium.

He reads *Paramahansa Yogananda*. Lying in bed, after taking a cold shower, a large white towel wrapped around his waist, he exercises his gums with a rubber-tipped metal instrument.

It won't take long for him to have someone. He won't have to take someone somewhere. That someone can come here and lie next to him on the queen-size bed. Lie. Together. When I leave, I'll take the dust ruffle. It was specially ordered from England. It cascades, in folds, to the plum-colored carpet. I'll take it. It'll remove the softness from the bed.

2. Friends

HER HAND MOVES THROUGH HER THINNING HAIR. HER EYES focus on mine and then she looks away. "I'm going to stop dyeing my hair as soon as it turns all gray," she says.

In the fading light of a humid August evening she and I sit on her terrace, waiting for the rain. The roses I brought lie between us on the table. The geraniums in clay pots haven't been watered and the terrace needs to be swept. Her neighbors tore down the wooden shed that separated their two backyards, replacing it with a chain-link fence. An attempt was made to spray-paint it dark green. "I should have planted ivy there," she says. "They could have at least told us. Bobby could have built something with the old wood."

In her right hand she holds a cigarette, in her left, an empty wine glass; her dexterity serves her well. Three bottles of red wine lie in an open cooler several yards behind us. I move to bring the whole thing closer and she says, "Don't. I need the exercise." And she gets up and peels away the wrapper from the neck of an unopened bottle and, calling on years of practice, pushes the cork down with her thumb.

She was a dancer with Martha Graham. Now her waist has thickened, her legs are thin, and the cornflower blue of her dress can't take away the weariness from her face.

Her mother called me last night. "Katya. It's terminal. Don't let her know I told you. Maybe she'll tell you herself."

With her glass refilled she moves her chair closer to mine, leans into the cushion, and says, "Why is Brooklyn suddenly on the way for you? Last time you said you were coming I cleaned the house and waited and you never showed up. This time you just drop in. I haven't seen you in, what? Three years? Next time I won't be home."

"I miss you," I say.

"Bobby made a Greek salad. Let me give you some," she says.

"How is it that you get husbands who cook for you?" I ask.

"I guess I'm just lucky." She laughs. "Are you and Phillip still together?"

"Yes." I recross my legs.

"When are you going to wake up and leave him?" she asks.

"How's Paul?" I ask.

"My brother is fine. You know he married her. Candy. Now she wants a baby and she makes him take vitamins to help her do it. He told her he had a vasectomy and she told him to reverse it. What? She wants to make a father out of him again at fifty-five? He has two with Ada. You have four with Phillip. And I have none with Bobby. What should that average out to? Two apiece?"

"Let me put the roses in water," I say.

"No. Don't. It'll rain soon and we'll go in. He's moved his company to Seattle. Bobby and I spent a few days out there. He's built this twenty-thousand-square-foot home that suspends over the Pacific. The master bathroom is as big as this house and it has a glass ceiling that if you touch one of the buttons it disappears and you see the stars at night. I asked him if he ever touched the button when there was a storm outside and he said that could never happen. Fourteen people can float around in the Jacuzzi that's surrounded by calla lilies and he takes the vitamins Candy gives him and throws them into the heads and says to me, 'Maybe they'll make them grow.' They're coming to New York at the end of the month, but he's not staying in Brooklyn with me, no, he can't do that. It's the penthouse at the Four Seasons."

"I wish I could see him again."

"You can't. She doesn't leave his side. He's lucky if he floats in the Jacuzzi by himself. I talk to him about you in front of her just to see her squirm. No. He's gone. Packaged. Done and gone." The strap of her dress falls off her shoulder and she doesn't bother bringing it back. "Did you notice my nose? I finally got it fixed."

"I never thought anything was wrong with your nose. What do you say to him about me?"

"I make things up." she says.

We hear the siren of a fire truck.

"I wonder how they maneuver these narrow streets?"

"Just like we all do."

The rain starts to fall and I reach for the cushions to bring them in.

"Leave everything."

We walk down the steps to the basement. She pulls out damp sheets from the dryer and I follow her into a room that is now a bedroom. Bobby lies on the unmade bed, their dog, Mookie, beside him.

"Let me help you make the bed," I tell her.

"No. Let Bobby sleep. Mookie threw up last night and when she did, I did. It was a mess. It took me hours to clean." And she drops the sheets in a pile on a chair.

We climb the stairs to the room that takes up the entire second floor. The windows are open at both ends and the breeze breaks through the smell of dust and cinnamon. She lights candles that stand on the sideboard, softening the light cast by the chandelier hanging from the sixteen-foot ceiling. She reaches into a cabinet and brings out an opened bottle of white wine; she pours it into a thin crystal glass, not caring that it's warm. We walk to the far end of the room. I sit on one of the couches that surround the glass table I had given her when Michael started to walk. She stands by the fireplace and from the mantel takes down an icon. She walks over and hands it to me. "I bought it in a village outside of Moscow. An old woman wanted five dollars for it, I gave her five hundred and still got a bargain."

It's old and it's covered by the tarnished silver *oklad,* allowing only the thin, dark faces of the mother and child to stare through.

"You should hang it," I say.

"Where should I hang it?" she answers.

"Above your bed," I say.

"It's not blessed," she says.

"I'll go with you to the synod and we can get it blessed," I say.

"Should I wait for you to come so we can go together? When did you become religious? Put it back for now."

On the mantel I see a framed photograph resting against the wall. It was taken the summer the three of us were counselors at a camp in the Catskills. Paul stands between his sister and me with his arm around my waist. We hiked twenty-five miles that day on roads that wove through neck-high corn. A cardinal flew low and I knew how happy I was.

"I didn't know this picture existed," I say.

"Paul gave it to me when I saw him," she says.

"He had it all this time?" I ask.

"Why are you surprised? Remember the dress you let me wear?"

White chiffon with small apricot polka dots. The slightest movement would set it in motion. She asked me if she could wear it to a party. I noticed my dress one Saturday, folded, in a laundry basket beneath a leaking bottle of bleach. Impulsively she cut her hair; she kept the long, thick braid in a box on the top shelf of her closet. I took her braid and wore it until it stopped being anything. She told me it wasn't an even trade.

"Do you know what I miss most? My hair."

"I know," I say.

"You do? How do you know? Your hair didn't go down to your waist and you didn't have a mother who spent an hour every day brushing it. All you had was a mother who told you my brother wasn't good enough for you. Who could amount to something. You threw my brother away like he was nothing. Like he was nothing. And you got Phillip. What a prize! Are you happy? You can't be. He can't make anyone happy. Happiness? And you knew Phillip and I were getting it on and you did nothing."

When did her eyes become lifeless?

"Say something."

"Let me have some of that Greek salad Bobby made."

3. Smile

MADISON AVENUE WAS WET AND COLD. THE fiRST SNOW OF THE winter disappeared as it hit the pavement.

Martin's wife said this wasn't a retrospective, just some photographs Martin put together for a show representing his work through four decades.

As I walk in I see Dooley. He and Leslie still live in the town Phillip and I left two years ago. Dooley tells me that it's always so wonderful to see me, that Martin and he went to Yale, that they and their wives try to get together at least twice a year, that it's always so much fun. I smile and say, "That's wonderful."

"You've lost weight, haven't you?" Dooley asks. I smile.

"I hear that you and Phillip are moving back to our little town."

I smile and know if he's heard this, he's probably heard the rest. "I guess you and Leslie are still together?"

His eyes quickly leave mine and we move our separate ways.

I stand before a large black-and-white photograph. A dark-haired girl sits, holding onto her cigarette. A boy, his head raised, lies beside her. The Coney Island boardwalk stretches out behind them into a summer haze.

"Isn't it amazing how close they let him come in?" a stranger beside me says.

"He was probably their age when he took this," I reply.

"Of course." The stranger laughs. "May I ask where you were then?"

"I was riding my bicycle to the library to sneak in to read *Nancy*

Drew and the Secret of the Girl Who Couldn't Remember. And you?"

"Stationed in Germany."

It's then that I see him.

He walks by, his hand holding hers; guiding their way through the crowd.

She's taller than he is, her thick, curly hair held together by pins.

A friend who knows her tells me he's cleared up her face. The same way he cleared up my weight.

I wonder if he tells her he is in awe of her? Does he serve her tea sweetened with rose-petal jam in his darkened office? And does he tell her, softly, to bend lower as he enters her from behind?

I move to the bar and a young man gives me my vodka with no ice in a wineglass and I make my way back to where I know they might be.

My hand reaches out and touches him on his deep blue cashmered back. "Hello," I say.

He turns and looks at me with no surprise. "Hi."

"Martin lives in our building."

"Who's Martin?" he asks.

"He's the photographer. We're at his show."

"You're still in the city?"

I turn and walk away and as I pass the stranger leaning against a pillar of that low-ceilinged room, I smile.

4. Birdseed

THERE WAS NO BIRDSEED LEFT FOR THE PARROTS, LORRITTA, WHO we've had for eighteen years, and Vanya, who remained with us after my mother died, and I drove the ten miles to the feed store.

I haven't been to this store in two years, ever since we moved out of our house in Westchester and into an apartment on West Eighty-sixth Street. Phillip said he could no longer afford paying for the house and the apartment and he was tired of paying New York City taxes and he's finished with trying to make me happy. It hasn't worked. So a month ago we moved back to the house that's surrounded by the pines and the quiet.

It was Phillip who had usually done this errand on Saturday mornings, either before or after the garden center, the dry cleaners, and the liquor store, the one that stands at the top of the hill. How many pounds of rabbit food did we buy through the years? Annie loved her bunnies.

As I walked in, the owner, leaning back in his swivel chair, his feet up on a stack of canned dog food, said, "Are you back? It's not what you thought it'd be. Right?"

I smiled and made my way to the bin where the birdseed was kept. The bin was empty; on the floor beside it stood an open sack of seed. He came over and we each filled a plastic bag.

"You've lost weight," I said.

"Actually I gained a little. I really lost it when my wife left two years ago. She ran off with an old guy she worked with at the electric company. This guy of hers put his wife in a nursing home and had my wife move in with him. Something happens to them, they sort of go nuts."

"Was your wife going through menopause?"

"Yeah, how did you know? Right. I guess you would." He laughed. "He died, this guy of hers. A half a year after she moved in. She's paying for it now though. Big time. She's taking care of her sick mother. Do you still have dogs?"

He and I walked over to the cash register and I took a wrapped piece of candy from a glass jar that stood by the hamster cages.

"She tried divorcing me, but it was lame and the judge threw it out."

"You don't want to give your wife a divorce?"

"No. She's not getting half of anything. She's really gotten old looking; she never took anything for it. And she's gotten to be afraid of things. Now it's the air bag in her car."

He followed me out carrying a twenty-five-pound bag of dog

food. He put it on the front seat while China barked at him from the back.

"Give your parrots broccoli; it's full of calcium. That way they'll live longer. Nice seeing you again. Take care of yourself."

5. The King Alfreds

CAROLE CALLED THIS AFTERNOON. SHE ASKED IF I'D GO TO THE ballet. She finally has a subscription and no one in her family will go with her. She'll pick me up, but I will have to drive in. She can't stand the maniacs on the road.

I know Carole won't come into the house and I know Phillip will watch her drive up. She avoids Phillip ever since George, her husband, came over and asked Phillip not to move the stone wall that stands between our properties. George and Carole buried both their Irish setters by it. Phillip pulled out the new survey that showed his property going beyond the wall into "land George shouldn't think is his anymore." George couldn't claim it, said Phillip, by using their two dogs as an excuse. And my husband had the stone wall moved. Now, fifteen feet of grass and two dead dogs are on our side of the stone wall.

I walk out of the house into a cold May evening. Spring is late this year, the dogwoods are just coming out. It will probably be a brilliant fall.

I wait for Carole to finish beating her car mat against the corner of the garage.

Carole hasn't lost her looks or the blonde in her hair. We both worry about our calcium. I eat cottage cheese and sardines. She takes Tums, three rolls a day. She doesn't smoke or drink coffee or eat any processed meat. She likes her champagne with a splash of raspberry vodka and she's wearing the black cashmere coat we flipped a quarter for at last month's St. Anthony's rummage sale.

She straightens up after putting back the mat and says, "I still miss the King Alfreds."

Carole is remembering the daffodils. It took us a week of afternoons to plant them. We laid the bulbs in five tight rows along the path leading to the playhouse. They came up stronger every May for fifteen years. When the new well needed to be dug, an underground spring was disturbed and it flooded the whole area where the daffodils grew.

I back Carole's Suburban to the front. I can't stop myself from looking toward the house and seeing Phillip sitting in his chair by the windows.

Last night, Phillip told me I was irrelevant to him. We stood a few feet apart by the stairs to the attic and he said, "Katherine. Don't you understand? You are irrelevant to me."

It takes only a few minutes to leave our country lane and be on the parkway going south. Carole unfastens her seat belt and says, "I don't want to get wrinkled."

I glance over to her as she begins to play with her hair. She'll take a strand and begin twirling it around her finger, using the twisted end, like a paintbrush, to dot her lips. She looks out the side window. "My mother had rosebushes. I wanted to dig them up from her yard and plant them where our tennis court used to be, but that cheap, miserable bastard sold them. She had a bush of blue ones. Roses don't smell anymore. They've strained the smell right out."

"Roses take so much time. I've tried covering them, not covering them. It doesn't seem to matter," I reply.

"Her roses grew from May to...November? There were roses on the table at Thanksgiving. Funny, I just remembered that."

"We always had a bowl of fruit on the table for Thanksgiving."

"She made the best apple pies. She'd have the kids pick the apples off the ground. She'd make six, seven pies. They'd be gone in two days. I asked her to give me the recipe. She'd say, 'Watch me.' I never was in the kitchen long enough to watch."

I thought of my own mother and all of the questions left unanswered.

"I'd have her out to the house in Shelter Island. She wouldn't be there two days when she'd say, 'Take me to the fruit stand. I want to get those peaches to make your father a pie.' A pie! When I saw the bastard take the bedpost and beat her with it. He kept it unscrewed and ready."

"Did she ever fight him back?" I ask.

Carole laughs. "Are you still hoping I'll say yes? I walked in on them once. He had her right on the kitchen table. He was mean. Mean. I'd ask him for a nickel to buy a Good Humor. You know what he'd say? 'Go earn it.' I was five years old. The only thing he ever gave me was a radio for my graduation and he bought it at the Salvation Army Thrift Store. And she had to die before him. He left everything, the house, the apartment buildings, everything to the archdiocese. He really thought it would get him to heaven. May his soul rot in hell."

"Rita Simmons died."

"I know. Finally," Carole says.

"They say she went down to sixty pounds. You could see her heart."

"That's not possible," Carole says.

"Yes. They say you could see it beating."

"Promise me, Katie. If I ever get that way, leave me off somewhere in the desert. Give me a sun reflector and tell me to just keep walking, that you'll pick me up real soon. Rita held on too long. There's a point where you've got to say, okay, that's enough. Thank you. Goodbye."

When is enough enough? Rita was president of the Garden Club. There were eleven of us. We'd pile into two station wagons and go planting around statues. Carole and I are the only ones left. Everyone else has moved away. Rita's husband was transferred to Keene, New Hampshire.

"I have to tell you the latest," Carole says. "I get a call from a dealer this morning. There's a show at the County Center. He tells me he's got what my husband wants. George has been looking for a BB gun like the one he had when he was twelve. His mother made him sell it. He got four dollars for it. Now, this dealer, how many years later? Has one just like it. In its original box, tissue paper, the whole thing. But now, of course, it's five hundred dollars. Today is George's birthday. Funny, he gets his wish on his birthday. He buys the gun, brings it home. By now he's had a few. I'm in the library, polishing the porridge bowl where I keep the gummi bears and I see him standing in the doorway, pointing the gun at me. He says, 'Let me just blow away that beaver. It's not doing me any good.' I tell him, 'Go ahead,'" and she laughs. "If only he knew where the beaver was last night, how wet and wild it was. I really cannot stand him. We did nothing for his birthday. I wanted to go to the Kittle House for brunch but he was out buying a gun. None of the kids showed up. Their father's sixty-fifth birthday. Can you imagine? I'll blow it away. It's not doing me any good." And she laughs.

"One of these days he might just do it."

"George? You know what he said to me? 'If I'd killed you when we still lived in Scarsdale I'd be out by now.' He's funny." She laughs. "Katie, what do I have? Maybe another five good years? As soon as we sell the house, I'm out. I'll get a house in Westport, on the water, close to town, where I can walk to everything. I can take the train to the city. I've had it with the driving."

"I thought you were going to Florida?"

"No. The whole state is one big air conditioner. I told you Frank is buying a house in Captiva. I'll make him open all the windows when I visit. It was so convenient having him so close by. Now? I'm really going to miss him. He says I'm like a river."

I wonder why they call it the Saw Mill River Parkway? There had to have been a river here. Once. Large enough to have a sawmill on it. Where did it go?

"Frank is the same age as George. Incredible. George can't get it up anymore. It's the drinking. It's sad. George was so good. Once. Still, not like Frank. It's also the genes. George's father left before George was born, so God knows what he was like. Frank's father is ninety and they have to restrain him in the nursing home."

I think how lucky Carole is that her parents died quickly. It wasn't very quick for my mother. But then she was with me and I held her when she died.

"The only problem with Frank is he repeats himself. He forgets and I don't want to tell him, 'Frank, I've heard this.' Listen, as long as he fucks me the way he does, I don't care. I put a smile on my face and say, 'Oh, Frank, what an interesting story.' He's a great cook, too. George remembers everything, when he's sober, which is not a lot of the time, and he can't get it up. Frank remembers close to nothing and can go on for days. Wouldn't it be great if I could splice them together and throw away what's not working?"

"With Phillip it's a mystery."

"Well, Katie, while you're trying to figure that one out, climb down those attic stairs of yours and join the world. Find yourself a man. All I have to do is put it out to one of Frank's brothers and you're in."

"I don't want that."

"I know. You want love. I was in Barnes & Noble the other day. I was looking through some books and I read something. It said, 'Love is something you don't have and you give it to someone who doesn't want it.'

"That's not true."

"Why are you holding on? Are you waiting for him to say, 'Katie, you're the best thing that's ever happened to me?' He's never going to say it. Get over it. He's incapable of it. Leave him."

"I am."

"Right. You'll be up in that attic of yours for a while yet. You've made it too cozy. And you won't let go. You keep your mother's ashes by your bed, for God's sake. And where would you go?"

"I'm going to U.C. Berkeley."

"To do what?'

"I am going to get a degree in archaeology."

"Being with one dead man is not enough for you? You haven't said anything to me about this. When did you decide this?"

"Last night."

"Last night? You're not serious. You're not going to do this. Anyway you're too old."

"I'm not. I'm doing it."

"It's too late to apply."

"I'm applying to the summer session. I'll be enrolled by fall."

"When are you leaving?"

"At the end of May."

"No you're not."

"I am."

Carole and I sit still watching the New York City Ballet perform *Sleeping Beauty*. A bar of dark chocolate rests in my lap. I try not to let the rustle of the thin foil be heard as I give Carole and myself a piece.

Carole leans over and whispers, "Isn't it magical?"

6. By the Railroad Tracks

THANKSGIVING DAY. PHILLIP MADE AN OMELETTE FOR FIVE, FOR himself and the children. I take China for a walk. She won't leave my side as we walk the old golf course overlooking the Hudson.

Phillip made reservations at the Kittle House for six at four. I'll sit between my two daughters, and for the first time in thirty years I'll eat turkey that I haven't put in the oven. Maybe I won't have turkey. Maybe I'll order goose.

I had planned Thanksgiving at home, inviting friends to relieve the tension.

Phillip told me that's not what the children want.

"Why?" I asked.

"Ask them," he answered.

I did, and they said he told them there weren't going to be any more Thanksgivings at home.

I planned to go to the Grand Union to buy eggs and toilet paper and instead I sit on a bench in a small park by the railroad tracks. I give China half my bagel with cream cheese. The car radio mentioned two Macy's balloons were damaged by high winds, one shredded completely, the other causing a lamppost to fall on a woman.

A black girl walks by in a camel-hair coat with a leopard print bag slung over her shoulder. Is it a mince pie or a plum tart in the plastic bag she's holding? Below me the New York City–bound train pulls in. The girl starts to run and I hope she makes it.

It's a blue, cloudless morning. The hardware on the empty flagpole beats against the metal.

A policeman walks over to where I sit.

"What are you writing?" he asks.

"My life story," I answer.

"Well, that's probably better than mine. Are you from around here?"

"The next town over," and I motion to where I think north is while telling China to sit.

"Where the snotty people live?"

"Yes, the self-important and boring ones."

"Brooding?"

"Boring."

"I'm from the Bronx."

"You know, there's not a person from the Bronx that I haven't liked."

"Yeah, it used to be a great place. They have a bunch of guys that take care of your town. We're all New York City cops come over."

"The pay is better here?"

"Nah, it's less aggravation. It's the aggravation that gets you. If you finish off your day without anyone getting killed or robbed, you've done your job. Anything else is an aggravation. Your first year, you want to help everyone. After twenty, you don't care if they live or die. It messes up your life. You bring your work home and your relationships suffer."

"You were married?"

"Yeah. She took off eight years ago."

"Did she run away with another man?"

"Maybe she did. Who knows? But she ran away with my daughter." He shoves his hands into the pockets of his sateen jacket. "That's enough to spoil your day."

"Have you seen your daughter since?"

"Nope. She took her to Italy." His eyes vanish as he looks into the sun. "What are you gonna do?"

"Have you remarried?"

From his jacket pocket he pulls out a blue photograph book

and hands it to me.

The first picture is of an infant placed in a pumpkin wearing a hat shaped into leaves and the second picture is of the little boy being held in his father's arms.

"Your wife takes very good care of your son."

"She does shit. I'm the one who cooks and cleans and she calls me a fanatic. Relationships? Relationships are an aggravation. The holidays are the worst. It's supposed to be a happy time and all it is is more depressing. You'd think it'd be your family that supports you, but it doesn't work out that way. It's the barber or the dry cleaning man or an old lady. They listen to you and give you support. Your father, mother, brother? Nothing. It's the people you don't know that give you what you want."

"Isn't it wonderful you have the kind of job that lets you be in touch with a lot of different people."

"Well, it was nice talking to you, I need to check up on the train station, see if they didn't trash it during the night. Are you married?"

"Yes."

"Happily?"

"We're separating." And it's the cold wind that's just made me shiver.

"Well, be good."

7. Rats

PHILLIP IS SQUEEZING JUICE FROM AN ORANGE WHEN I WALK into the kitchen and without looking up he says, "Are you aware of the twenty-one-thousand-dollar bill your lawyer sent me? Why don't you get a job and pay for it?"

"I have a job."

"Why don't you get a job that earns money?"

"My job eventually will."

"Fuck you."

Using both hands, he brings the glass of juice to his lips. I decide to make a poached egg for myself. Waiting for the water to boil I again tell him to get an exterminator. We have rats in the basement.

"Michael and I put poison down."

"They're too smart for poison. Why can't you just call an exterminator?"

"What do you think an exterminator is going to do?"

The bell rings. The big, bronze ship's bell that was hung to the right of the front door by the admiral who had the house built in 1907. He named his home "The Anchorage."

"Are you expecting someone?"

"Kormandy."

Phillip must have called Mr. Kormandy to get an estimate on the damage done to the ceiling and the garden-side wall of the kitchen when the pan he was frying french fries in caught fire.

"Mr. Kormandy, you don't have to take your shoes off. Nobody else does."

He smiles and extends his hand and wishes me a happy and healthy new year and continues to untie his laces. He's not as thin anymore and his dyed hair makes his face look older. The last time he was here seems so long ago.

"It is holding up," he says, looking at the rooms as he stands by the staircase.

He doesn't know we had someone else after him. Someone recommended by the contractor. If Mr. Kormandy had done the painting maybe we would still have our doorknobs.

"Mr. Calt. How are you, sir? I was saying to your wife that my job still looks good. How long has it been?"

"Awhile," replies Phillip, remaining seated. "I take it you've been well?"

"Actually, not so good. I married again. A twenty-year-old girl that I got from Hungary."

This must be his fourth wife.

"She bought fifty-nine pairs of shoes and filled two closets with clothes. In two years she spent twenty-five thousand dollars. I knew she would be a girl with problems; her father was an alcoholic. He told his children he would throw them out of the window so she is a nervous girl. I thought when I brought her to America it would be okay. She bought a six-hundred-dollar dog and she does not pay rent. I have to divorce her. I met a girl in Hungary. She is different, but who knows? Maybe they are all the same. I want to marry her."

The pot I was boiling water in is burning and I remove it from the stove. I look at Phillip. He sits and eats raw cashews from the bowl I keep filled.

"Does your wife work?

"Oh yes. She has a very good job cleaning houses, and I got her a green card so she is okay."

"Did you buy Amazon.com?" asks Phillip.

"No. Did you?" and they laugh. "But do you know what I have been buying? Museum-quality paintings in Budapest for two thousand dollars. I have thirty-two paintings. I think it is going to be very, very good."

"Mr. Kormandy, while you're here, would you look in the sitting room?"

He interrupts me. "It's that outside stone wall. I will see how bad it is." And he leaves Phillip and me alone.

In a lowered voice Phillip says, "I'm on a limited budget. I'm not having any extra work done. You got that?" And his eyes become like two ink spots.

"Get an exterminator. I saw a rat coming out of your room."

8. By The Clock

I'M TO MEET MY LAWYER IN GRAND CENTRAL BY THE CLOCK. HE and I will walk to Phillip's lawyer's office. It's been ten months since the four of us have had a meeting. Nothing's changed. Phillip and I still live in the same house. It's now a question of who moves out.

I'm taking the train into the city. I won't have to deal with the traffic or the expense of midtown parking. I've given myself fifteen minutes to walk down the hill to the station.

A light rain has started to fall. On my way to the coat closet to get an umbrella I see part of the ceiling lying on the piano, the Steinway grand Phillip bought Anne when she was eight and asked her father if she could learn how to play. I told Phillip there was a leak in the master bath shower and he said all we had to do was reposition the shower head so that the water would fall right into the drain and wouldn't collect along the sides where the leak probably was. I guess the ceiling couldn't take it anymore. The plaster is wet and I've got to get it off the piano before it stains it and I've got to cover the piano with something that's waterproof in case the rest of the ceiling falls. Do I have anything large enough? Maybe I should roll the piano out of the way? No. Then the plaster will fall on the wood floor and stain that. What should I do? I'll move the piano. I'll lay a couple of blankets that I still keep in the closet from the time the children used them and the cushions from the couches to make teepees.

I barely make the train.

The conductor asks for my ticket.

"I didn't have time to get a ticket."

"How much time did you have?

"Five minutes."

"That was enough time. I won't charge you the two-dollar penalty. Next time get your ticket at the station."

I notice a young man sitting diagonally across from me. I had seen him on the platform while I was catching my breath. He's so clean. He has a new suit on. Everything he's wearing is new. Does he shave? He must. I'm not near enough to know if he uses cologne. Probably. He's still talking on his cellular phone.

"I'll figure it out." "You know what?" "The truth is." "Profit." "You know." "I'd buy it." "Sure." "Exactly." "No rush." "As long as it's in our possession." "I'll call you when I get to the office."

A thick gold band encircles his left ring finger. They probably bought one of those prefab modular homes starting at $790,000 on Hardscrabble Road. Did they choose to have it assembled on level ground or on a knoll? They have two acres to landscape. In the fall they planted fast growing pines to obliterate the view of the neighboring power lines.

I think of Lillian Hellman. Her farm was on Hardscrabble Road and this new development is part of her farm. Her farm, where she grew bleached asparagus and raised poodles. I was in her farmhouse once, now owned by friends of friends. I sat in the library where she wrote and I was shown the linen closet where the shelves have been left labeled MISS HELLMAN and MR. HAMMETT. She sold the farm to pay for Dashiell Hammett's defense. She didn't have a choice.

The young man sneezed. A balding man in a pin-striped, white-collared shirt says, "Bless you."

"Thanks."

He's coming down with a cold. He's overworked and he goes outside with wet hair.

He stands up and goes to the doors as we pull into 125th Street. The doors open and he gets off.

Of course. He's one of the ones who is going to make Harlem presentable.

I pretend not to see Phillip in the building's lobby. We take separate elevators up. We're all right on time.

"The tuition for the Columbia University course Katherine is taking is completely unaffordable. To the extent that she wishes to pursue adult education, the budget should indicate the cost of classes at Westchester Community College, within reason of course, not Columbia University or a comparable college," says Phillip's lawyer. She looks smart wearing a size two beige Calvin Klein suit, ticking off at $350 an hour, Elsa Peretti's gold misshapen heart dangling from her throat.

I wonder who paid for law school.

"We'll get to that. First, I'd like to discuss Katherine and Phillip's living situation. Phillip should move to an apartment in the city. Katherine and Stephen should live in the house while Stephen is still in school, which is for another five years, and then, if Phillip wants the house, he can buy Katherine out."

"That's unacceptable. Katherine hates the house. Has always hated the community. She's stated this time and again. Phillip loves his house. Let Katherine be the one to rent an apartment in the city. She should live where she has always wanted to live. Phillip works in the city and he loves coming home to the fresh air."

"Stephen is in school here and Katherine stays with her son until he graduates."

"Let her rent a house."

"Katherine is not renting a house. If Katherine moves it will be into a house of her own. This is non-negotiable."

"Katherine is well aware there is no money for her own house."

"The Nantucket house can be sold."

"The Nantucket house is for Phillip's retirement."

"You know very well, Nancy, if this goes to court there will be a division of property, and aren't we here trying to avoid court at all costs?"

I wonder if the rest of the ceiling has fallen down.

"An agonizing fifty-thousand-lifetime cruise through the hell worlds is what they had to look forward to."
(Perry, page 155)

Winn-Dixie

Jeffrey Skinner

Like an intelligence test for the weary,
these isle marquees–would Kleenex come under Paper Products,
or Cosmetics? Shortcut through Breakfast Cereals.
Pass a boy in a shopping cart jump seat, holding out
a silver 'Vette, thumb-sized. He's around three,
brown hair cut straight across his forehead,
still able to wander into a story by Grimm,
get lost between the forest and goodnight. "*This!*" he says
of the car in his butter-roll fist. "*Yes!*"
I answer, "I *know*!"–You don't lose that boy language.
At the dairy case I'm struck dim by milk
light, and the miniature anxiety of American choice—
eleven varieties of shredded mozzarella. Settle on Wisconsin
All Natural Partial Low-Fat Semi-Dehydrated.
The teenage cashier is pretty, in that hopeless teenage
way, laying the receipt and change across my palm,
smiling like a dopey saint. Drop receipt,
walk out into dinner-hour hush. Cross the parking lot
past Skyline Chili. The bell for six-thirty mass
rings from St. James, and the early
fall light's beginning to thin: faint blue
smudges a fringe of trees. Take the back alley home.
There, a man I recognize from a Walker Evans photograph
jigs toward me, his body a rubber lure
spasmed ahead by transparent lines
rising from his head and left shoulder.
He tries to look at me, poor fuck, but his eyes and face

are locked in different directions. Fear
if he hits me up for change I will crumple
to brick, offer him my house, my car, my life. Our faces
turn from each other like opposite magnets.
Back home, late, as usual...My wife, who is also blameless,
snatches the vacuum-sealed packet from my hand.

Survey Says

Jeffrey Skinner

There's no money in predicting sadness.
Late at night, beyond the cricket's raspy *giddyup,*
I hear cars go by like enormous whisk brooms.
I don't know a thing about the people sealed inside.

Once I looked at human faces and thought
I could see thought, crossing: a ruffle
of wind over water. But I've lost that. Not
all loss is bad. The abandonment of trees

as metaphor, for example: *men walking as,*
inhaling the dark, etc....No money in that either.
Survey says: Optimistic people are happier.
But the pessimistic are more often right.

A friend was making the usual precarious
living, balancing angels on the head of a pin,
when he suddenly got the idea to clean up
the streets of America. He moved

to L.A. and wrote crappy movies to finance
his gifted scheme. I called, said Hey, what about
those streets? "I think I'll write crappy movies
a little longer," he said. He sounded well.

I'm a bad citizen. The only extinct
species I care about is me. I hear things late
at night, and it isn't America singing, pal. It's more
the grinding of some axle, the cricket's *giddyup*.

Video Vault

Jeffrey Skinner

You like movies, you're an unusual guy,
you cruise past Foreign because you're tired,
you've worked hard and don't have it

for subtitles and missing plots and pouty
French nymphets with no earthly analogue,
you run into Dan in Horror, Hey, what's that?

—some stab and maim but you've seen it,
you don't want to chat, later for Dan
(but, *nicely*; it's a small city...); you check

out comedy, you've seen the funny ones
three times each, why do they make
comedies that aren't funny? On to *Tough*

Guys, a little vicarious physical justice
always good for a lift before sleep,
Clint, Sly, Arnold, Steven, Chuck, etc.,

pounding hell out of some featureless battalion
because, you know, they pissed him off...
you've seen the good stuff there too,

so on to Drama. Gummy, yellowed
boxes, the actors' ties and hair all wrong,
huge. You should write a movie, dammit!

What would it be about? *Two misfits fall in love*
against the odds and...A man sets out
to avenge his...In the not too distant future...

Other movies, that's what your movie
would be about. The thought depresses.
You know there's nothing you want

in New Releases—everyone's desire
is the same...The average day demands
imagination, and what you really hunger for,

even in two dimensions, is a vision of
another dimension, *Wings of Desire,*
for example, where angels hang

in libraries, reading over mortal shoulders.
Of course, it doesn't end well. You don't know
how to say it: You need a tongue

of pictures, something to lick away hours
spent on contracts, difficult clients. But
it's getting late. You can't find *your* movie

anywhere. You drift off, become a fly
landing at random on boxed images,
and the titles grow illegible and huge, like

some system of absurd canals, or patterns
left in English wheatfields overnight.
Humans sifting by appear as gods—

distant, irritable. And you, with no voice...
What *is* that smell, a mix of yeast and popcorn
and mold? *Here, sugar. Here, sugar sugar...*

The Good Sportsman, Et Cetera

Guy Lesser

THE REAL PROBLEM WAS NOT KNOWING.

That T. was going to be on the New York–Milan flight via Rome, scheduled to arrive at 10 A.M.—but now posted three hours late—had been Gray's assumption for several days. Now he was not so sure. Certainty was vacillating once again, as it had been since Friday had come and gone without her calling to confirm the details.

He'd already phoned her too many times earlier in the week and left too many cheerfully empty messages on her machine. It would not do to call again. So, he'd waited, imagining the phone would ring at any moment. Imagining what he'd say. How he'd radiate reassuring charm and uncomplicated pleasure that she was finally going to come and visit him in Italy. But she didn't call. And by 6 A.M. (only midnight her time), he knew she wouldn't.

Thursday, when he'd broken down and tried again, he'd reached someone who said he was her "service." This was, he guessed, a kind of news, though when or why she'd gotten a service in addition to her answering machine was a riddle. It seemed to beg endless, obsessive, slightly paranoid questions about what he didn't know (or at least no longer knew) about her and her life and her friends, especially the new and male ones.

"I still haven't gotten my ticket," she'd told him Wednesday, "but they said they'd send it tomorrow." He could hear the genuine excitement in her voice. "I don't know which airport, but I know it gets in at ten."

The crowd milling about the arrivals building had grown gradually through the morning, as expectant groups joined impatient ones awaiting half a dozen flights unaccountably delayed. Los

Angeles–Milan–Delhi—one hour; Sidney–Singapore–Karachi–Milan—five hours; Rio–Milan–Rome—twenty-five minutes; Chicago–Milan–Dubei—three hours thirty minutes. The effect, as Gray ultimately worked it out, pondering the great mechanical black-and-white board dominating a bland, postnational lobby of stainless steel and molded plastic, was that all due and overdue flights would arrive at Malpensa in a single twenty-minute glut. The neatly planned and efficient spread of safety-conscious half-hour gaps had collapsed, a figment of some wishful computer's fantasy.

It seemed a much smaller airport than Milan would deserve. Two simple, contemporary buildings with a bit of sprawl between; a single pair of frosted electronic doors for the incoming transcontinental flights; a short row of competing automobile rental kiosks, each displaying a distinctive combination of eye-catching corporate colors. Overall, it seemed a poor first glimpse of Italy, a marked contrast to the neorationalist, Gothic-Assyrian splendor of the central railway station built by Mussolini in the thirties. It seemed, in turn, so much less majestic than the entry into Italy most travelers would have known fifty years before, traveling in a diligence drawn by a team of horses across the Alps.

He tried to imagine the jingling of harness bells and the sound of horseshoes meeting rock and ice, the smell of snow caught in a glittering gust of fresh alpine air, and the first moment, when, rounding a curve and finally heading downward, one would see the first farms of the southern valleys coming into view.

They had met in a club a little more than three years earlier. She had been with an artist he knew named Mitchell whose early work had consisted of spray-painting menacing silhouettes on dark walls in unlit streets, and whose later work consisted of large, spare canvases of dark horizons spanning calm black seas. They'd talked. Gray thought she was the prettiest girl he'd ever seen. And she thought Gray was huffy and arrogant and looked mean. Then, about a month later, Mitchell had brought her to an opening, and at the dinner afterward, they'd sat next to one another. So, it was okay to ask her for her phone number. Which he did.

They went to dinner a week later. And afterward, they went to the Yale Club for drinks and stood on the rooftop terrace, trying to discern some pattern in the windows still lit in the Graybar Building. Their arms touching, but only barely, she told him the only thing she had ever liked about modeling—which she had given up to go to business school—was how they brushed the makeup on your face with sable brushes, while you just sat there, your eyes closed, listening to music.

One night, they'd seen a really horrible Italian movie, full of social and political pretense, trying hard to be outré and avant-garde. The best scene involved an act of fellatio, several minutes long, performed seemingly in time to a lush, nineteenth-century, vaguely Russian-sounding overture. As the music built, the movie's hero, an idealistic young Sicilian auto worker, made vaguely sexual noises while paraphrasing an eyewitness account of Lenin's first triumphant entry into the new revolutionary capital of Moscow (this accompanied by rather badly coordinated English subtitles).

And so, somehow, later on that evening, what had been in the air all week was made flesh. They had their own sex scene. Starting in the kitchen doorway, a slow damp kiss unwound, and the weeks that followed seemed wondrously uncomplicated.

A milling crowd, more than a dozen deep, began rapidly to converge along the barrier in front of the frosted glass doors leading out of Customs. For at least ten minutes nothing else happened, then, suddenly, passengers wheeling luggage and luggage carts and carrying flight bags began to surge across the threshold, occasionally interrupted by small guerrilla-style bands composed of grandmothers and sons and second cousins who periodically leapt forward, over or under the barrier, unable to contain themselves a moment longer.

Maybe if Gray had actually planned to remain away a year, his feelings and intentions toward T. would have been, or would have had to have been, clearer. But he hadn't, so they weren't. He had tried, at least since January, to fall in love, hoping maybe that might force him to resolve things, but though there had been a Norwegian furniture restorer, an English girl who did trompe l'oeil at Spinelli, a recent graduate of Bryn Mawr learning a fussy, complicated academic style of portraiture that involved marking the floor with tape and endlessly measuring distant space with bits of string, it hadn't really worked. And Gray found himself invoking T. rather consistently in his conversation, and wondering what she'd think of things he saw, and ultimately, really for the first time, he found himself thinking of T. in that most conventional of terms, The Girlfriend He Had Back Home.

Sometimes he thought that maybe the real problem was that in leaving everything unspoken, nothing was really wondrously uncomplicated. It was simply more consistently ambiguous and treacherously vague. Not very different from being an unevolved, unhip, less arty long-distance couple—just less clearcut in useful ways. Promises that weren't made were expected to be kept, and expectations solid as concrete always floated on the most unpredictable of ethers. And what about the freedoms that one had supposedly retained—to do however one pleased without apology or explanation? These always seemed to leave him with an oily feeling. Not quite guilt, exactly, rather inchoate regret that he had added unnecessarily to the growing fear there would soon be little left to the wondrous, undefined them. Which, as T.'s voice and scent and laughter began gradually to fade and meld with those of other girls he knew, saddened Gray.

He was glad that she was coming.

Though there was much about which he was feeling edgy. This time he was resolved that they'd start fresh. He'd be patient with her in ways he'd never been. He'd try to make her feel she was important to him. He began to imagine how once they were comfortable in the day-to-day routine of being together again, without every transatlantic second having to count or cost so much, that once all the myriad intangibles one forgets had been patiently reassembled, they might begin to really talk. Maybe, just maybe, he hoped, they could, for the first time, really plan whatever was to be or not be.

That was, of course, if she was still coming, which he didn't know for sure, since she hadn't called to confirm.

At that moment, he saw her struggling through the crowd with two black cloth bags, her clothes not ones he knew but everything else perfectly familiar—especially once she smiled, a smile he knew was really genuine. Bashful. Almost. And as the kiss they exchanged over the metal barrier, midriff high, unwound and grew more complicated, he knew, he was certain that everything was going to be just fine. He knew, he felt entirely sure, that everything was going to be fine.

Shortly after 5 A.M., as the sky began to shift from luminous blue-black to a faintly illuminated lead, Gray lit the first cigarette he'd smoked in several weeks. An instant little friend with a tiny orange halo, silent and warm and undemanding. T. was downstairs behind a locked door, asleep insofar as he could tell, with all the lights still blazing. All quiet after the storm, too, was Gray, gazing at the landscape, listening to the slight contrapuntal harmonies of waking birds. He didn't quite feel sorry for himself so much as badly beaten up, wondering if maybe he was simply much too sensitive to anger. Knowing finally and clearly that it was over between them, but also not knowing what should, or was going to, or even what he wanted to happen next.

He had never actually heard her scream before. Or anyone, if he thought about it.

Two brief *eees* had been the signal of unendurable distress. Compared to cinema's more familiar, souped-up realism, it was difficult to believe they signified anything very terrible. The sound blended in, like real gunfire or the thin stuttering-engine whine of an animal being slaughtered, the moment after the sound had passed.

But he could feel the house was different now, filled with the inaudible vibration of quietly mounting dread.

"None of your friends really like you," she had assured him fairly early in the spiraling devolution of the evening. The rage behind this and the extremity of each of her subsequent contentions had only grown worse, in an accelerating rhythm of ever-loosening constraint. Like the act of sex, he thought, seen from the outside, there was something ridiculous about the way lovers fight.

"You don't really know," she said, "anything. You don't know anything about me really. The only reason I came here was to show myself that I had finally grown strong enough to deal with all the ways you twist things." It was as if she were searching for something, anything, that would get under his skin. There was, he knew, some truth to her saying she'd come to test or exorcise him, but then he also knew her signs of showing she was happy with him. And the confusion she felt about him now wasn't very different from the confusion she always felt about caring for someone who wasn't much around and who didn't have an awful lot of money and who wasn't glamorous or good looking or famous or incredibly important. When he'd tried calmly to ask her probing questions, she'd reacted with an infuriating singsong voice he thought he recognized. "Maybe. Maybe yes and maybe no—I don't really have to tell you anything." But even this, the more comprehensible section of the fight, sounded silly and melodramatic in recall. As he played it back and smoked his cigarette, he thought the lines had not really played well even when she was saying them. They had less the emotional intensity of great feelings inarticulately expressed than the affecting pathos of an unhappy child mimicking with childish dignity a parental fight heard repeatedly but not yet fully comprehended.

It was what she said afterward that had frightened him, as she revealed beliefs that seemed to ring with the harsh, clinical jangle of genuine pathology. She had demanded that he open his hands. "Open them," she said over and over as he sat on the bed beside her. "*Open* them." It had confused him horribly. He began wondering helplessly if he should hit her. Not from anger, but from the growing fear that cooled and trumped all anger, that her panic was growing hysterical.

She had thought, she finally told him, that he was holding a knife.

It made the moment strange. It made the moment sour and black, but not enough to laugh, which was odd, since laughter had always been his shield against everything. But it was the last thing she said to him that really stopped him cold—about how she'd always thought, from the day she'd first met him, that he was someone who had killed—a murderer. And it had been that which had attracted her.

At the railing, along the brief wide avenue that runs beside the Arno, between the Ponte Vecchio and Ponte alle Grazie, Gray stood next to T. They were gazing at the wide, flat water between the bridges, and the buildings wavering slightly, watching the reflections on the hurrying but unfaceted surface, which in the gradual summer approach of sundown was slowly shifting hues from a neutral range of grays and jade to crimsons and vermilion.

Below them, a fisherman stood on a tiny patch of shore between the river and the rusticated stone embankments.

"Does anyone ever catch anything?" asked T., evidently trying to be pleasant.

All week long, men Gray didn't know had been calling her—making and unmaking plans which he half heard, for rendezvous in New York, definitely, and sometimes, for Milan or London. One of them, he now knew, was paying for her company.

He looked at her standing next to him, trying to imagine how she looked to other people. Twenty *maybe*, not twenty-eight; almost Coke-ad, beauty-queen pretty, and with just the right, healthy hint of moderate athletic enthusiasms. The perfect girl. Everything any boy could ever want. He imagined her veiled in bridal white, but he found himself recasting the mental image as a glossy magazine cover—her breast obscured by leaders announcing the secrets of "Seven Honeymoon Heavens" and her head crowned with a one-hundred-point italic word invoking the blissful syllable of either brid- or wed-.

The fisherman's rod bowed slightly. Gray wondered if it meant more than twisted line.

What did it mean to know someone or to be together? Especially when everything consisted only of what the other person said? There had been a girl that Gray had known once in New York. She had believed—at least it was fairly certain after he had known her a while, that she believed she was a Rothschild. She talked endlessly about her uncles and their houses and horses and wines. She talked about who she loved within the clans, and who she hated, and what they'd done, spinning tales of dark, labyrinthine plots, and counter-plots, and secret counter-counter-plots. Her passions were always grand passions, her friends always true ones, and her gestures always drawn from the unlikely terrain between a bubbly 1930s Christmas fantasy and Suetonius's *Lives of the Last Roman Emperors.*

"You are a great artist," she would tell Gray. "You must let me buy you somewhere beautiful—so you can work. I am going to look at some flats tomorrow—you must come, so you can choose."

A case of Mouton or Lafite, which never came, was always on the way, usually in thanks for some small kindness, like a lift home in a taxi, or a twenty-dollar loan.

"You must tell me the year you were born," she would demand, not a little imperiously, "so I can tell the warehouse." Then he would tell her his address for the umpteenth time, and she would repeat it, very slowly and distinctly and loud, as if by doing so she would be fixing it all the more indelibly in her memory.

What was odd to Gray, especially as he began to grow more skeptical, was the way that *everybody* accepted her for what she claimed she was. Not just the scraping, obsequious maître d's addressing her as "Baroness," but virtually every seasoned beau monde New Yorker that he knew and thought should know better. "I'm not really sure," they'd say, or "E. never said a word about nieces or nephews, but I'm sure he must have some." Even the former flames of verifiable Rothschild cousins and the scions of families with long-standing Rothschild connections didn't seem to know anything one way or another. The irony of all this, Gray was sure, was that she would probably have been quite as popular without the masquerade. There were times when her charm and her beauty could captivate the entire room.

Then one night, she threw a dinner party for a famous writer. This was held at one of the restaurants of her true friends. Twenty people, six courses, four wines, none a Rothschild, and the next day, she disappeared for good.

Gray had puzzled over the moral of the experience. It had something to do with madness, and how we perceive or fail to perceive each other, and trust (not just the simple questions about the mutual indiscretions we trade with others to bind a friendship, or the necessary joy of living some part of our days with our guard completely down, but also all the more threatening and intimate and basic questions about how much faith one can ever dare put in one's powers and instinct for self-preservation). None of Gray's puzzling, however, would ever resolve itself into anything that was prescriptively very clear or remotely useful. He had liked her. He enjoyed the ease he felt in talking with her. And he loved the playful intelligence they had almost always managed to spark in one another—no matter what they did and no matter where they went. This had survived, without any noticeable impediment, long after Gray had grown fairly sure his suspicions were correct. Sometimes, when he thought about the idea of her, he wondered if he was showing good character or no character in continuing to be happy in her friendship. After she was gone, and the last, lingering, hopeful uncertainty had fled, he felt the way you feel when you've been robbed or your apartment has been broken into. A little hollower, somehow. Maybe a bit more brittle, and older.

The arc of the fishing pole had grown noticeably more taut. The surface of the water was broken, only a few feet distant, with a small, sharp flash.

At the end of an affair, Gray realized, a version of you dies. Sometimes, it is an especially nice version that no one else had ever managed to bring out in quite the same way.

He knew now that there had never been anything very tangible in his love for T. That it had not proceeded like a syllogism from first causes or good reasons or the march of history or the plan of fate or God, or even the comfort of habit or the burden of inertia.

As for the making sense of it, he knew there were always plenty of facts at hand. Thousands, reasonably well sorted, on every subject, ranging from food allergies to the names of childhood pets to a fairly detailed knowledge of each of her eight or nine most major boyfriends. (The first had been a half-Romanian dance instructor in Roanoke, Virginia, who liked her to wear short dresses and real stockings—she was sixteen and he enjoyed making love to her in front of his friends.) Gray knew not only the most shameful secrets of T.'s family (though he had never met them), but also everything they'd ever thought of him, along with everything that T.'s analyst and T.'s voice coach and T.'s aerobics trainer and each of T.'s best friends had offered as advice about him and their vague, long-distance involvement. But in the end, he realized, it was all more or less irrelevant. It all boiled down to liking the person he became with her, and the person she became with him. Laughing at the same stupid things. Not having to finish most sentences. Sometimes the feeling seemed powerful enough to trounce anything. Maybe it wouldn't cure insanity, but it could certainly deal unhappiness a mighty whack.

In the fragile normality of the week following his cigarette, Gray found, however, the old ease had chilled, as if he now knew too much for both of them to be quite comfortable. Half his jokes seemed to go quietly awry, and when he'd touch her now—even in a restaurant or walking down the street—he would feel less pleasure than a kind of subtle, near-wifely mix of mild resentment and resignation.

"Look!"

But he was already looking.

He saw the flashes were clearly now a fish trying to outrun the line. Flight, with an ever-shortening radius.

There was a patient sureness and correctness about the fisherman that communicated itself even to T., who watched, frozen, aware that the fisherman knew exactly what he was about, and that the contest's key moment was by now long over.

"Poor fish," said T., holding Gray's arm. "Poor fish." She clung to his arm, almost as if searching for something. Every nerve tensed, as if she believed he could swoop down like an angel to divinely intervene. There was something very small about the way she said "poor fish." Something that made him want to cry or put her head on his shoulder and stroke her hair until the last hint of evil in the universe had perished.

Brought up into the air with a net, the fish and its last futile agony of flips could be observed quite clearly even from the distance where Gray and T. were watching.

Then, even if he couldn't quite take credit, Gray knew exactly what was going to happen.

Though she didn't really believe him until after the hook had been dislodged and she had actually seen the fish pause bewildered, and then swim, none the worse for his experience, away. And for that moment there was a visceral tenderness between them, watching the scene resolve like a parable. Half spell, half romance, half happy movie ending. The Good Sportsman, et cetera.

"Rather like you and me," said Gray, finally ending it, knowing he was summing up her year too well. In the momentary pause before her laughter, good full laughter this time, in which all the year's tensions were banished and erased, he could feel everything was suddenly changed again, though all she actually managed to say to him was, "Oh, Gray."

And during the few remaining days of T.'s Italian sojourn they often returned to the moment. It was the sort of moment one could never forget, she said. But he knew she would forget, before she was off the plane. That it was the sort of moment impossible to record in either its simplicity or its complexity. And that what could not be recorded adequately or thought of clearly couldn't really be remembered. It had contained everything that they had ever really liked about each other, though.

And still later, when he knew he was going to be all right, after his sense of her began to fade, he would wonder if maybe she wasn't the fisherman after all, but merely the bright, glittering lure.

"I tried your phone number once or twice, but to no avail. I figured you might be jet-setting."
(Bolton, page 197)

Days of Or

Adrian Dannatt

THERE IS SOMETHING ABOUT THE OAK BAR AT THE PLAZA AS afternoon light starts to dim down into evening that brings reassurance to even the most justifiably agitated. It is as if the setting within and the waning without merge into a solid mood that unites interior and exterior, dark walls and somber skies acting together to neutralize the soul. It is so sad, so redolent of wasted hours, those hours that slowly, mysteriously become wasted months, lives, that it cannot but cheer.

Sherban watched darkness mount and was content. He had just finished lunch and was enjoying a last Armagnac in contemplation of leaving. Not that he actually intended to leave for some while. Dusk came early and he knew from experience coldness and wetness came with it. Here everything was inherently toasty, burnished and agleam as if rubbed down daily by gold bullion wrapped in brown velvet. His host, Marcus Friedman, had left him with a relatively rare Bolivar to smoke and, more importantly, an open tab at the bar. In exchange for paying for everything, Friedman subjected Sherban to a detailed acount of the dreary machinations of his job. Marcus hated working for his father, who in return didn't seem much keener on his son's employment. Conversation revolved around whether Marcus should leave, when he should leave, and his incapacity to do so. Clearly this was not very interesting. It was only because of the cruel paradox that Sherban loved the atmosphere and ambiance of expensive restaurants but did not have the means to pay for them that he partook of such talk. How much more entertaining life could have been if Sherban had not been born with a lust for antique paneling, private dining rooms, discreet service. If he had never developed his craving for obscure wines and seasonal truffles he would not have to listen to a whole range of boring things. Oh, for a diet of toasted cheese and the company of those he found amusing. It never occurred to Sherban that he himself might work, make money, save and scrimp and thus afford to buy his own dinner, that perhaps he could even eat alone at his favorite table in the city, with a book propped proud. But between the boredom of a job and the boredom of having to listen to other people he chose to endure that which provided the more immediate form of gratification.

"Another, Professore?" Strange that the barman still thought of him as a distinguished academic—a mix-up over visiting cards stretching back to his days at Yale Law School.

"Grazie, Paolo." He took the glass in his palm, feeling the warm liquid through bowl and stem, letting the acrid flavor haunt his nostrils. Savored like this, one glass could last till nightfall. He assumed Marcus had not set a limit on his tab, yet it would be embarrassing to find out differently. Sherban had nothing in his pockets but a subway token and one very large crisp banknote, sadly of Ukrainian denomination. How he disliked the messiness of attempting to leave a bar and being asked if he could "settle up," having to explain that it had all been taken care of earlier. When you never carried money, like the British Royal Family, every transaction became a minefield of potential hostility. It made you acutely aware of how every deed or venue required a symbolic exchange of cash. Going anywhere, doing anything depended on a series of tiny tithes and small bribes, a network of nodal points at each of which money was required, like medieval town gates. If you tried to get through a day without spending a single coin, the sheer number of these monetary checkpoints—fiscal barriers—became painfully apparent.

Sherban yawned, impressed that he could be almost as boring in his freedom as Marcus was in bondage. Every time they met it was Sherban's role to sympathize about the impossibility of working at Friedman, Friedman & Friedman and to suggest alternatives. He had already come up with an exclusive cabaret on the top floor of the Chrysler Building, a documentary film production company in California, an upstate New York vineyard, and a pleasingly loss-making publishing house. Each time Marcus brimmed with excitement, scribbling strategy on the back of his Hoare's checkbook (a year at Oxford had led him to favor British banking) before going back to his job for another decade. Sherban was quite as aware as Marcus that none of these alternative jobs would ever be realized. Marcus would carry on working for his father and complaining bitterly about it for as long as he, the father, lived. It was just as well these other plans were strictly theoretical, because most of them would have involved Sherban.

He was too polite to refuse any offer of employment. "But would you really be able to come into an office every day, could you see yourself getting in on time in the morning, working late?"

He was always being asked these questions. Every time he reassured Marcus that indeed he relished the prospect of employment, regular hours, a fixed salary, and good Lord, maybe even a health plan.

"I've been lingering in the margin for quite a while now. Actually, not even the damn margin itself, but rather those holes in the margins where the file binder goes. It's time I got back onto the main page, write myself into history, y'know."

Why did he have to pretend he wanted a job when everyone knew it simply wasn't true? Merely his perverse obedience to some archaic law of social obligation. Luckily those weekly offers of screenplay collaborations, book editing, PR positions, and curatorial assistantships, the usual flotsam of the churning cultural machine, always neatly faded away.

Instead he was alone in the luminous gloom of the Oak Bar, among the last of the lunch guests, or was it the first of the evening crowd? Alone he admired the falling, fallen darkness and skeletal trees of the park, the tone of his Armagnac, and the way it held the very last of any light in the room. Sherban enjoyed his solitude and proud record of unemployment at another day's end. But he was aware sadness lurked right outside the door, the dismal weather of reality, the drizzle of dailiness that would surround him.

The best to hope for was that somebody he knew, a friend of a friend, an acquaintance of an acquaintance, would secure his passage through the rest of the evening. These things were tricky to arrange, the precise mathematics of chronology and cost. He had been at the Plaza since twelve-thirty. Marcus had insisted on an early lunch due to business, leaving for Sherban a tricky gap to be straddled between afternoon and evening sessions, an hour or so during which he would be lost without sponsor, patron, or alibi, adrift in this bar awaiting providential synchronicity.

"Are you waiting for someone, Professore?"

The barman was an expert at such delicate issues.

When someone sat in the same place doing nothing, it took decades of waiterly experience to tell the difference between those who wanted to stay and those who wanted to be prodded into action. Paolo remembered the Professore had once performed some amazing card tricks, dropping the pack onto the floor "by mistake" but predicting the order they would land. Moreover, the Professore's guest that evening had been someone of singular importance, both familial and financial, to the hotel. This florid young man of importance, with the red cheeks of a schoolboy and an appropriately enthusiastic manner, had confided in Paolo, drunkenly, "You know this chap is the most extraordinary genius, degrees from every university, Ph.D.s and diplomas pouring out of him, absolute first-rate mind, and never had a job in his life."

Paolo was suitably impressed; he would have been so whatever this man said.

"No job, never! Not a single job. You know how he makes a living?"

Paulo shook his head as required, ready to be awed.

"Card tricks, nothing else!"

For Sherban this had indeed been a brief phase, a sticky patch that lasted no more than four months, though his memory retained the rusty stain of certain tricks. He had met an Iranian backgammon pro who in exchange for lessons in the seduction of American females gave Sherban the ABCs of card feints. All you needed were the standard tricks, a banal repertoire, and then everything else depended on bluff, blarney, and myth. Sherban had been fairly inept at the tricks themselves, but his look had been convincing: seventies Dior tinted glasses, sockless, faux Gucci loafers, a naval blazer with verdigris on the buttons, and a cowboy shirt featuring diamonds and aces.

Such history stood Sherban in good stead with the barman. Thus Paolo happily let him slip down from his barstool without a tip and with a couple of drinks technically not accounted for.

Sherban weaved across the room, expecting at any moment to be brutally shot in the back with a cry of, "Signore? The check!" He was not steering well, being drawn toward occasional tables as if by magnetism, the doors ever distant. He turned to wave good-bye to Paolo with dignified cordiality—a risk—but the good man was back at work polishing glasses, awaiting the evening crowd.

He wandered through the lobbies of the hotel and stopped off in a kiosk to flick through the *New York Review of Books* to see how various acquaintances were doing. He had difficulty concentrating on the contributors' notes. One friend had gained tenure, but Sherban was not in the mood. Academic rituals seemed too distant when he was faced by the cold facts of a winter night, the slush and streets awaiting him. Sherban realized he was shirking, malingering, refusing to confront what lay before him. He felt a chill pass through him, the lightning strike of doubt that he had dreaded for years. He knew how nerve failure began, with the smallest ball of insecurity, and how it spread, paralyzing all one's resources. It was a gray mold, a shadow, that crept up from within and occupied the soul, leaving one with all the tics of bonhomie but incapable of a single smile. As with top salesmen, Sherban had known of legendary installment-plan spielers, fêted county-club dragueurs who one day, after thirty years of aplomb, find themselves a little reluctant to make even one more cold call. They put it off, don't have the right number, need one more coffee. And when they head back to the phone there is no longer any hiding from the fact that they have lost the confidence they once had. They cannot summon the nerve to make any more such calls, though they have done so every day for decades. One morning like any other and the jig is up, the job is over. Because even when you have plucked up the courage to make that call it will never work as before, because everyone can smell the fear; the greasy anticipation of failure fulfills itself.

Sherban had in the past left the grandest and warmest of

hotels with relief, feeling free from the conventions of the toasted-muffin brigade, a surge of optimistic intrigue at what might come next; whether better or worse, it would at least be different. Yet now he loitered in the Plaza lobby in a manner that might eventually alert security. And what a truly preposterous hotel to find oneself stuck in, as if the Plaza still retained a shred of mystique with its vulgar Monopoly money status. How long had he been lost in these yellow corridors, a lifetime of prevarication stumbling up and down the rococo dog day looking for exits? It was the shame in even visiting such a hotel, let alone lingering, that drove Sherban to action. He pulled his coat tighter, cupped hands to savor one last time the memory of Armagnac, and strode outside.

It was clearly beastly out by even the most optimistic salesman's estimation. Not exactly sleet or drizzle, but a cruel mixture of the two adjusted specially for single people whose shoes were not well soled, cold wind with a cunning horizontal approach that no umbrella could successfully resist. Dusk for good now. But the steps of the hotel were beautifully lit, proffering a warm welcome, and even though they had so obviously been designed to create a gleaming 3-D advertisement, a blatant, vulgar marketing gambit, they still could not fail to entice. The doormen in their uniforms with big umbrellas, the reflected sheen of water on diamond paving, polished rails, the creak of revolving doors, how could one have the strength not to return? Plunging his hands into his pockets, Sherban was delighted to encounter the thumb stub of a cigar. His luck was changing. He'd forgotten the half Davidoff Churchill he'd plucked out of an ashtray at the Yale Club last night. He'd been slightly embarrassed when he realized it was still lit. Minutes later a man had returned to his armchair with a cognac and, after adjusting bifocals and finding his place in Gibbon, had reached blindly, absentmindedly, for his cigar, letting his fingers roam over the ashtray. Sherban had left the room trailing smoke from the pocket of his dinner jacket, a jacket that had already seen a great deal of combat over the years. He now placed the chunky stub of tobacco in his mouth, feeling rich again. Under the awning of the hotel in such tedious meteorology, things were not so bad.

To think this had once been his favorite place. To smoke a

cigar watching the storm bucketing down, the gold statue looming through the mist like some promise, the prow of a ship of wealth and beauty, where once he had stood drunk with the potential of this city—a Noah's Ark of impossible breeds, a freighter weighted full of hope. Now he was waterlogged, a tramp steamer, stamped teamster, beaten back to port.

Sherban crossed to the other side of the steps, as if zigzagging back and forth might grant the courage to launch forward. He approached a lady of perhaps, just, her twilight fifties under an umbrella decorated with leaping cats. Her head scarf, tight as a turban, was similarly decorated with prancing felines and she smoked a cigarette with singular dedication.

"I don't suppose you have a light for my battered old Churchill?"

She glanced at him sideways, a suspicious squint, looked him up and down.

"My husband knew Churchill, he even went to visit him in Washington during the war. Something to do with intelligence work, it was never fully explained."

"Probably encryption. The best minds were set to work on encryption," added Sherban hopefully, taking the cigar from his mouth.

"I don't think my husband was one of the best minds. He was a number cruncher, as they used to call them." She made no indication of reaching for matches.

"They still do. The city is full of number crunchers. They take the best apartments."

There was a sadness in his tone, but he persisted. "Number crunchers did much encryption."

"A Churchill is also the name of a cigar, named after him presumably?"

He agreed and lifted the tip to the flame of her lighter, a veritable petroleum Shiva that danced this way and that in gusts of wind. The demi-Churchill glowed slowly.

"How extraordinary." The woman was staring at Sherban's feet. He shifted them with a certain shyness. Could their odor reach that far?

"My husband, whose wartime record we were just discussing for no apparent reason, had exactly the same pair of shoes.

Identical."

"Correspondent?" he ventured, turning them this way and that now with pride.

"Two-tone we called them then. He bought them on one of our trips to Panama and, I have to be honest, I was never quite sure about them. Well, I mean, in his case..."

"No, no." He waved away her blush. "I know exactly what you mean. I've also had my doubts, serious doubts have tortured me some mornings. But they are the only ones I have..."

Sherban immediately regretted this tone of self-pity.

"I mean, of course, the only two-tone shoes I have. The only pair like this."

But the woman was not to be fooled. Her expression was now severe, staring down.

"Show me your right foot again, I just saw something." He obliged.

"There! Stop! Just as I thought. What is that?"

And what was he expected to say? A unique design feature, special aeration?

"It is a hole, isn't it? A huge hole!"

She seemed happy about the whole thing, as if she had just proved something.

"I have a hole in my soul," admitted Sherban.

"A hole in your sole must be repaired."

She stamped out her menthol filter with the determination of a new beginning. "This may sound crazy, but I simply cannot allow you to walk around in the rain with such holes in your shoes. It is my duty to stop you from catching pneumonia, make sure you have adequate shoes."

"That's awfully sweet of you, really..."

She put a hand up to halt him, imperious as a dowager arresting a postillion.

"I should put my glasses on and inspect you properly. One's always hearing these awful stories about serial killers." She adjusted her spectacles and nodded approval.

"Entirely presentable, as I first thought. What are you supposed to be doing now?"

"Doing?" Sherban looked bewildered. "Well, I didn't really

have plans as such, I just thought I might saunter around for a bit, get my bearings..."

"You'll be doing no sauntering, young man, not in this weather and those shoes. You're going to come home with me, I'm just a few blocks from here. I'm going to find you a pair of shoes that Saul never wore. What size are you? Nine? I knew it, exactly the same as Saul."

Sherban suggested she had better things to do than look after the shoes of a complete stranger.

"Nonsense, I just had an endlessly dreary tea with the cousins from Dallas. I really shouldn't bother with them at all, and I was just wondering what to do with myself."

The doorman hailed a cab, tipped his cap with a smirk.

"I hope they don't think I'm rustling some young gigolo back to my place," she giggled. "Do you think they noticed the way I picked you up?"

"I don't think anyone would mistake me for a gigolo," Sherban reassured her, a certain poignancy to his tone. "I fear I'm really rather past my sell-by date for such things."

"Nonsense." She looked ahead. "A little battered perhaps, nothing a night's rest won't restore."

They drove in silence and descended outside a large apartment. Sherban made the shuffle toward his wallet, having long perfected the right rhythm between eagerness and tardiness.

She took hold of Sherban and asked in a whisper; "Are you, by any chance, Jewish? "

He grimaced. "I'm all sorts of things just like that and even more. Not practicing all of them."

"Of course not." She seemed jubilant. "I didn't think you were a Jew, which makes it perfect."

She swept him into the elevator and to the tenth floor. Sherban was insulted at having his putative Semitic heritage so briskly dismissed, but this was how she wanted it and he never took offense. The apartment was everything he had been expecting, serried shelves of knickknacks, windows clearly not opened for years. Sherban stifled a yawn, so overpoweringly sleepy did it make him. She led him into a storage room and astonished him with the late Saul's shoe collection, a trove of brogues, golfing shoes, and Cuban heels lined up like a Hollywood wardrobe department.

"The only things of his I couldn't bear to throw away. Help yourself, please."

For these were the Days of Awe, the High Holy Days. His hostess, the redoubtable Mrs. Goldstein, believed in the *sefer ha-chaim,* the Book of Life opened for each individual on Rosh Hashanah, closed and sealed on Yom Kippur, and influenced during this interval by acts of contrition, repentance, and forgiveness. Acts of generosity, especially to goyishim, ensured an impressive entry in her book. In her study he found a full-page advertisement placed by followers of Rabbi Menachem Schneerson. Whilst waiting for Redemption everyone should do everything in their power to bring it about by acts of kindness and charity. There was one paragraph marked with pencil that announced, "Indeed anyone, including you, could be responsible for the one caring act, that special gesture, the charitable gift which tips the scales in our favor and brings Redemption to all mankind." Sherban, it seemed, was the charity case who might tip the balance of the world toward Moshiach, harmony, prosperity, and knowledge. This certainly made him feel better. Not least about Mrs. Goldstein's future phone bill.

It was not disheartening to think that he might be personally responsible for a forthcoming paradise on earth. Bring on the messiah, he muttered, bring him on and let me go home.

Springtime

A Comedy by David Robbins

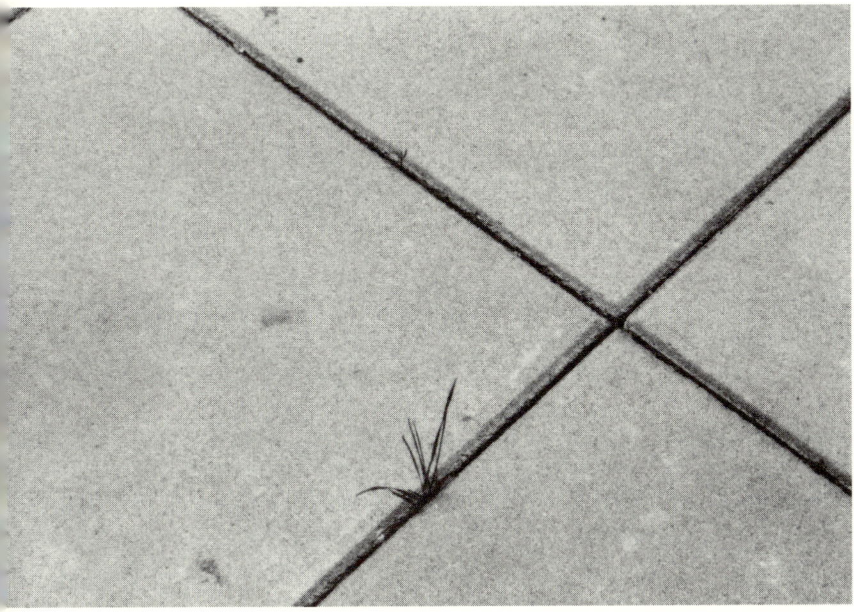

"Why do I believe,
at age fifty-two,
that by spraying
Yves Saint Laurent's
Rive Gauche near
the open window of
my attic bedroom,
it will replace
the smell of my
first cigarette of
the morning?"
(Zaitzeff,
page 45)

Photo by Serge Corriera

Police Blotter

A Year In Crime '98

Phnom Penh, one hell of a town! On the following pages *Open City* examines the sliced, open underbelly of Asia's most sordid city. It's The Best Of: A Year in Crime on the streets of Phnom Penh. Poisonings, throat slashing, kidnapping, grenade explosions, and whores galore. So wade into the mayhem.

Excerpts courtesy of the Phnom Penh Post, *summarized from several Khmer newspapers by the honorable Michael Hayes.*

Shy Minh En, a Taiwanese businessman, was injured by confused military and civilian police as he attempted to escape from gun robbers who had shot at his car. He was reportedly very afraid and drove to a checkpoint for help near the Olympic stadium, but officers mistook him for a robber and shot at him. He then fled to another checkpoint for help, but when the military and civilian police caught up with him, they stole $3,000 and his hand phone.

Kim Run, 22, was wounded on his penis after his wife Noun Sim, 19, tried to sever it after becoming enraged at his requests for sex.

Kim Run said that his wife agreed to sleep with him only five or six times in their nine-month marriage. He added that his wife had disappeared from home several times but he did not suspect that she had a hidden boyfriend. On the night in question she agreed to have sex with her husband but had hidden a blade to cut his penis when she touched the penis and the penis was becoming enlarged.

Three drug smugglers were killed and two arrested by the anti-drug police near the Lucky Supermarket. Two of the dead men were killed in an exchange of gunfire and one committed suicide by exploding a grenade to his head so that his head was blown off. Police seized five thousand amphetamine tablets, three pistols, and one motorcycle. Sources said the men were all criminal police originally from Pailin. Note: Pailin is a former semi-autonomous Khmer Rouge stronghold operating in Northeast Cambodia and currently harboring the majority of Khmer Rouge leaders.

Try Sem, 39, and her son-in-law Ros Ron, 18, fled away from home after they had love with each other. Sem's daughter, 18, said she got married to Ros Ron three months ago but her mother got pregnant by him four months ago. She said her mother had not allowed Ros Ron to sleep with his bride since the marriage and claimed that the mother faked illness so that the bride and groom had to look after her and could not go on their honeymoon.

Moto driver Yorn Lyna, 27, fell unconscious after two passengers invited him to enjoy drinking ABC beer and eat duck eggs laced with poison in the park in front of the Cambodiana Hotel. The offenders escaped with his motorcycle.

Claude Mathe, 56, a Frenchman, committed suicide by hanging himself at a room at the Singapore Hotel in Phnom Penh. Nobody knows the reason for the suicide, but a source said maybe he had a mind crisis.

Leng Vanny, a pregnant woman, and two of her children were killed by their cruel husband and father who cut their throats with a knife after he came back from a drinking place. A source said the offender attempted to kill his entire family but luckily one of his children was in school and his mother-in-law was at a pagoda, otherwise all would have been killed. The offender was arrested.

Police arrested a crippled man who attempted to take the gallbladder of a three-year-old girl by disemboweling her. The girl's mother shouted for police after the man had cut her daughter's abdomen open.

A monk at Wat Langka was found with nearly five kilograms of Burmese heroin that police said was bound for Vietnam.

An unidentified person was found dead, his naked body bound by the arms and legs, and a gash in his back where the gallbladder was removed. Note: Some Cambodians are known to roast the gallbladders of their enemies and eat them with rice wine.

A girl, 16, was rescued by police from a brothel in the Toul Kork area, to which she had been rented six months earlier by her natural mother for $30 per month. The girl's stepmother informed police of the young girl's whereabouts. The victim confirmed that she was initially rented to an old man as a virgin for $450 for two days.

The upper and lower halves of a murdered woman were found in two separate places in Phnom Penh. The lower half was found first in Toul Sang Ke. The upper half was found the next day in House #449E1, Kampuchea Krom Bvd. Most of the sources suspected that the body was Chinese.

Em Kosal, 27, a student at the Faculty of Medicine, strangled himself to death with an electric wire after he earlier unsuccessfully tried to drink poison. His sister said Kosal lost more than $30,000 while gambling at the Holiday Casino, Phnom Penh. Note: The Holiday Hotel Resort and Casino is partially owned by Cambodia's President of the Chamber of Commerce, Theng Boonma. Boonma, reported to be Cambodia's wealthiest tycoon, is barred from entering the United States. He is suspected of being one of Asia's largest transhippers of heroin.

Two policemen, Prak Sam and Lin Hun, were shot and killed by another man at a Phom Penh theater. Witnesses said the three men loved the same prostitute.

Phal Sopeak, 14, had his left eye smashed by his neighbor. Sopeak, who sold peanuts, said the offender had eaten the peanuts without paying, and when he tried to stop him was attacked. Doctors at the Ang Duong hospital said they would waive the $70 fee for removing Sopheak's eye and replacing it with a glass one, because he was so poor.

Yargn Loem, 42, and Pov Sarun, 39, were arrested by police in Tuol Kork after they had tried to catch a dog in a big bag. The two said they sold the dogs they caught to a restaurant for up to 20,000 *riel* each.

An unidentified moto-taxi driver was killed and his passengers and another moto-taxi driver were wounded when a mine exploded at a Phnom Penh market. Police said that a woman was riding on the moto-taxi with a mine in her plastic bag that exploded.

Sok Sarray, 26, who residents reported often undressed herself along city roads, and her husband, Sok Vorng, 27, were arrested while trying to steal a motorbike from a man. Saray confessed the acid she was carrying when arrested was to rub into the face of the moto-taxi driver.

Ly Phally, 39, was arrested by police after she attempted to poison a schoolgirl and then gouge out her eyes. The offender confessed that in 1996 she and an accomplice gouged out the eyes of five people to sell them for $400 a pair. Police are searching for the accomplice, a man named Phal, who pretended he was monk. No one knew who bought the eyes.

Translated from Khmer by Bou Saroeun

Welcome to Arcadia

Fred Leebron

ONE

I CANNOT STAND IT HERE ANY LONGER. THE PEOPLE ARE IN A socializing frenzy, asking each other to dinner or tea. I did not come here for company. I came here for solitude. We should live in separate caves and meet only at restricted times—not for dinner and never over tea.

We all live here to be different. Some of us are more different than others. Otto says it cannot go on like this. He occupies the hammock in front of the grocer's. In the winter he has only his long beard and tweed overcoat to keep him warm. He will not come live with me. I have not asked him, because I know he will refuse. He is so big and full of paranoia. I love him.

When I worked at the bakery he loved me, too. I gave him fresh bread for free. The work was hard, though, from two in the morning until ten at night. No one wanted to have fun. They only wanted to make money. Money, money, money. We were supposed to be a collective. Arcadia was supposed to be a commune. None of it happened.

Oh yes. We all made the same money at the bakery. We overcharged and cut costs whenever possible. It made me a little sick, but the people made me sicker. Everyone wanted to make the bread "really nice," make it look good, so it would sell well. The pastries would be sprayed with swirls of chocolate and vanilla, topped with strawberry caps and pineapple rings. The French bread would rise an arm's length and look as golden as sunstruck sand. It would all taste like cardboard. They only thought of selling. Baker whores.

I quit and went to see the Big Man. The Big Man has office hours at Woodstock every afternoon from two to four. He is a shriveled worm of a man, obscured by German shepherds and Doberman pinschers.

I waited my turn. It was in the summer and the stench of piss was foul. Loud music rang in my ears, and by the time I got introduced, I could not hear myself think.

"Let me see your hands," the Big Man said.

I laid them on the table like pieces of ivory. The dogs ignored me.

"You can always tell a man by his hands," the Big Man said. "Where are you from?"

I told him.

"If you are caught the worst thing will be some days in jail and then deportation. Scare you?"

I shook my head, but it did. I had been here for a year and hadn't left Arcadia once. I didn't know whether I could live outside it. But I shook my head.

He told me something about how much I should sell, and that he would keep his eye on me. He did not scare me. There are only a thousand of us living here, no escape from anybody's eyes. The favorite pastime is gossip. At the bakery, after money, it was all I ever heard of conversation.

So I've been pushing for another two years...But here, what is time? Old Otto doesn't even know how long he's been here.

Today is like any other day. The tourists are everywhere. Old people out for a stroll, high-school expeditions, undercover policemen. They treat us like an open-air museum.

But we are more like a town after a bomb has dropped. Most of our buildings lie in ruins. All of us suffer weird traumas. We have no lights for the nighttime.

In the winter bonfires burn on our streets.

Our violent fields heave in fruitless humps.

The main throughway is a broken road of bottlecaps and cobblestone.

Piles of trash are heaped everywhere.

For Fuxaid.

Incidentally, my mother died when I was two. My father drank himself silly in bars. I left home at sixteen. It is easy to make it around the world without money. Many people are willing to exploit you. I lived with a painter for several years, whose main objective was to wrestle with the snake in my pants.

I searched for places as bleak and as full of possibilities as the night. Kathmandu was full of chickens. I got lice in Ladakh.

All the women wearing mittens…

All the men sucking cock…

Only Arcadia held me, swallowed me like my own revelation. Drugs helped. I did lots of them, all kinds. Never was an addict. Could stop any time for however long I felt like it.

The Big Man likes me.

"I trust you," he said the other day.

"I sell well," I said.

"That, too."

I am charmed by his mangy appearance. He wears a 1940s black pin-striped suit and purple socks. His shoes are beat-up loafers missing the tassels. Shirtless and with silver wings of hair growing on the sides of his head, the Big Man does not aspire to anything but money. But he does not live here, either. He lives in a whale of a house in the city. I have eaten dinner there twice—Pusher of the Month honors.

The Big Man likes Otto, too. They enjoy sharing lunch and a chillum. Sometimes I watch. The Big Man grunts. Otto talks in sentence fragments, mostly nouns.

"Disgust Sin Devil The Fun Is," Otto says.

The Big Man nods. Maybe they are talking code. Otto is so big he can talk anything.

I love you, Otto.

Love is like a sailboat full of wind, cutting across the sea, soaring to the stars. But as soon as it lifts off the water, it belly flops down. That is what love is like.

We are sitting on a picnic table outside of Moonfisher. Otto is explaining life.

"Christ Sins Thorns In My Side," he says. "Jews Man Lifeboats."

His voice rings like a gravel pit.

Won't you hold me, Otto. Please?

The Irish priest is here again. I see him running past the grocer's, being chased by his flock. Even the Irish live here. They own farms and grow potatoes that look like bull's testicles.

"Repent!" the priest shouts out of breath as he runs, not daring to turn. The sun makes his black frock sheer, and I can see the nipples of his breasts.

"Fuck you!" the Irish scream. The men wear beards and the women have licorice hair. Every month the priest returns to claim his flock, and every month they drive him back into Copenhagen. But he never gives up. Some day, I think, he will inspire a crucifixion.

There is too much religion in the world. Personally, I aspire to internal spirituality. Nothing, nobody, outside of me matters. Except Otto. Otto is as religious as I get. His aviator cap is like a halo and his tweed overcoat is the vestment of a new savior. But there is too much talk about religion and not enough talk about faith. I, too, am full of anecdotes but without one developed plot. For Fuxaid.

TWO

EVERYONE WANTS TO KNOW WHAT IT IS LIKE TO LIVE IN ANARCHY. Let me tell you, it's no big deal. We all have daily routines, postures, objectives that supercede idealized anarchy. And the power grabbers make sure that there is more "we rule" than self-rule.

I am generalizing. Sorry. I realize this place has its virtues. Otto could not exist anywhere else. You cannot go howling sentence fragments all day out in the real world without somebody arresting you. But in here you can.

And me, could I exist elsewhere? Probably not. As I said, the real world is not the place it used to be. But in here, in Arcadia, it is strange enough. Too much happens—that's true. And often people here subsist on an incredible self-love. They feed on their egoism as desperate wolves caught in a trap feed on themselves. But Arcadia is where I live. It is a comet in the sky, falling fast. It is like eating too much candy. It is drugs and farms and pastel colors til you puke.

It is the child of civilization.

Today, the Uro came. There were sixteen of them, marching in rows of four. They kept in step. I was watching from the secret alcove with a couple other pushers. We were laughing and ordering all the dogs to attack, but they ignored us.

We stopped talking when we saw Otto. He was making for the Uro like a drunk polar bear.

"Good Christ Jesus Praised Be Uro Lord Vice," Otto roared.

I tried to shut my eyes but couldn't.

"Clay Dung Human Crap Uro Smells Of—" But their clubs knee-jerked from their sides, and Otto subsided to a growl. When they were finished the mouth of his silver beard had turned purple.

The Uro slinked off like bad children. I rushed out to Otto, crumbs of hash trailing in the cobblestone.

He was laughing, his teeth smeared vermilion and his lips like raw meat. I tried to clean him up. He bellowed something unintelligible.

I was crying. My tears made his nose run. The other pushers giggled. It began to snow. I was making a mess of everything and people were laughing at me.

I am hiding now in one of the abandoned munitions dumps, my knees drawn up to my chest, warming myself in the dark.

No one will come look for me. No one cares about me.

I want to be alone.

I need to be loved. What does it feel like?

You can cry so loudly that no one will hear you. Or you can whisper so softly that the whole world will come to comfort you.

Otto lies in the Health House, breathing like a gravel pit. Many people attend him. The Big Man nervously twirls his gold watch. I know it. I see so well in the dark.

I would masturbate if I could. To be so fully alone like this, the goose pimples rising up and down my arms. It makes me hard.

I am almost happy.

I sat with Otto in the Common Kitchen today. He scared all my clients away, but I did not mind. We had our own table with a lit candle stuck in a wine bottle. Sometimes I held Otto's hand without him noticing.

It is a hand like a shell on a beach, cracked but smooth. I took it to my ear and the roar of the ocean washed over me. Otto was cursing.

I dropped the hand and it swatted me on the breast, chucked my chin, then swiped my beer. Otto is a devil.

I hang out in the bakery to keep warm.

The Baker Whores are busy. Christmas is coming. Jens speculates that they can make a lot of money. When he is not looking, I steal a ten-crown coin from the box. Then, as he goes to deliver bread at the grocer's, I give him the coin and ask him to buy me a pack of cigarettes. He says, okay.

The bell rings at the shop window. No one else here; I have to answer it. One of the bikers wants something. His arms are lined with graying tattoos, and his thick waist is ringed by a leather strap studded with metal balls.

"A Berliner," he says.

I give it to him.

"How much?"

"Five crowns," I whisper.

He gives me five crowns. He is a member of the big gang. They never used to pay, but now they occupy a house in Arcadia and are trying to be responsible. They look like they're in pain.

Jens comes back with my cigarettes, and I excuse myself.

The Full Moon party yesterday at Arne's was awful. Everyone wore a costume but me. I went for the booze. Otto stumbled in later, wearing his aviator cap. He looked himself and everyone comforted him. He roared his regrets that he could not come, even though he was already there. They all laughed and started plying him with Full Moon Punch—a biodynamic cocktail containing homemade alcohol.

Half the people were dressed like David Bowie, smoking clove cigarettes. No one talked to me. I hung on the fringe of the circle surrounding Otto, and drank the punch from a styrofoam cup.

Some of the Baker Whores did start to approach me, but I sneered at them. They're looking for more people to work the Christmas Market. Not me.

After midnight, in the spirit of things, another pusher offered me a bargain on mushrooms and I accepted.

I ate them right there. Soon my insides began to roar and heat rushed to my face. I thanked the pusher and slipped out for a walk.

I stumbled out to the ruins and listened to the Greenlanders standing around an open fire, passing whiskey. They are pathetic people with faces like walruses, and I like them a lot. But they smell of piss. I can stand them only in the outdoors.

They had a chillum and I ingratiated myself by filling a round. They continued to ignore me, which was reassuring. Some of them fondled loose branches as if they were weapons, but they were not violent. Besides, I am my own dog.

They talked dialect and I stared at the flames. Cracklings popping over our heads felt like fireworks. In the distance we heard the idle roar of the party.

I reached for a new sensation. I reached out to touch a walrus's cheek, and that started the fight. I got a kick in the gut, and as I lay there looking at the night a pack of bikers drinking in the fields swooped down to kick the shit out of the Greenlanders.

Before I could get up I passed out. The next thing I knew, a biker was dragging me away before the Uro came. He said one of the Greenlanders was dead.

The ice ridges of the fields ripped open my back. The biker said I was leaving a trail of blood, and he cursed me.

Lights filled the field and he dropped me.

I fell into my darkness.

THREE

I AM LYING IN A CITY HOSPITAL BED, LETTING MY STITCHES REST. A policeman occupies a nearby chair. When I go to the toilet, he goes, too.

They found several hundred grams of hash while undressing me. I am to be deported as soon as I can be moved. I get to choose which border. They have no knowledge of my homeland, because I ditched my passport and I refuse to speak.

The ceiling is false cork and white. Counting all the pockmarks is like trying to count the stars. The ceiling has twelve different subsections over each bed. Each subsection contains hundreds of pockmarks. Each pockmark is one more hole in the universe.

They say I am malnourished. It is all the Full Moon Punch going to my liver, never stopping at my stomach to fill it up.

I have lain here too long without visitors. All civilized people have visitors.

"Do you play cards?" I ask the policeman.

"Don't tempt me." He sneers through a mound of facial hair.

"May I borrow your newspaper?"

"You're tempting me." He rises from his chair.

Already I can feel his club working up and down my legs, sweat pouring from his brow, a tight smile on his beard.

"Go ahead," I say. A warm chord runs through me. I will wet myself if he does.

But a group of policemen enter the ward. They are grinning. One waves a small packet. Terrible news. They have unearthed my passport.

I belong to an important country. I have a passport like a credit card. All the other countries accept it. For Fuxaid.

I am in Hamburg in the Hafenviertel. Hamburg is a nice place once you get beyond the train station. Maurice, a vagabond from France, cuts my hair. I have already shaved three times today. My train leaves in four hours for Copenhagen.

"Don't lose my identity," I urge Maurice as he clips away.

He shrugs. "Isn't that the purpose?"

I ask him to come with me. He refuses. Sometimes the whores from the Reeperbahn come down and give him a free one. Hamburg makes him very happy, he says.

"Except the train station," I laugh.

"The train station," Maurice looks at me gravely, "is the best part."

He takes me to the Hauptbahnhof. We descend secret stairways to a murky canal. Beneath the tracks, old men are racing swans. Their feathers gleam through the sludge.

"Care to bet?" an Englishman asks.

"Never gamble," I say. I place five marks on number nine, Riding Hood.

Riding Hood wins. I give it all to Maurice. We dash back up the stairs and I make the moving train.

Goodbye, Maurice.

How many times have I sat on a train approaching a border, queasy and tense with the fear of being detected? This time, however, I am my own illegal baggage. I do not want to go to jail, but I cannot be away from Arcadia. So I take this risk. They need only to computer-check me to find out.

First the Germans. They look at me and see my passport and nod and grimace and generally act like idiots. But the walkie-talkies hooked on their belts remain unused.

Here come the Danes. They are big boys in their black winter coats. Why do so many Danes wear beards? Maybe they are trying to hide something from themselves.

I feel myself giving way. I want to shout, Take me, take me, just let's get it over with. My tongue flaps inside my mouth, my asshole puckers out to kiss the seat cushion.

The hairy Dane fondles my passport. His bulk fills the compartment door, and I have no place to flee.

Then I think of Otto. This always brings me calm. My hands rest on my knees, seeping sweat. The scarf around my neck weighs like a sacred cloak. Otto has come to me, to save me. My head is as light as a snowflake, and flurries off my shoulder to the window, to regard the Danish countryside in all its boring splendor.

The fucking Dane stamps my passport. I am free, free forever, free until caught again, free as no man can be, free like the snow in the air.

I am in Denmark.

House Detective

for Kenneth Starr

Geoffrey O'Brien

Only when the flashgun
registers the couple
on the bed still hotly embracing

even as their heads
swerve involuntary
toward the invading light,

only then—the passkey
clutched in his fist, the payoff
tucked firm in vest pocket—

can he afford to lean back
in the doorway of the love nest
and in sweet relief breathe out.

Signage For a Four Story Building

A Project for *Open City* by Liam Gillick

1.

2.

3.

4.

"Six thousand cigarettes, seven hundred cups of coffee, nineteen tubes of lipstick, the collected works of Erich Fromm."

(Walser, page 141)

Introduction to Daniil Kharms

M. E. Yankelevich

DANIIL KHARMS (1905-1942), BORN YUVACHEV, WAS FIRST ARRESTED in 1931 on the grounds that he belonged to an "anti-Soviet group of children's writers." Kharms, who had at the time of his arrest become popular as a children's author, was the leader of one of the last avant-garde movements of Russian modernism, the OBERIU, or Union for Real Art. The OBERIU's three leading members, Kharms and his two close friends, the poets Alexander Vvedensky and Igor Bakhterev, made up half of those arrested in this group case. The OBERIU was at the time being targeted in the Leningrad press for its uncompromising, genre-breaking performances, which included proto-absurdist plays, film montage, pseudo philosophical debates and recitations of zaum *(trans-sense) poetry and the group's own brand of alogical verse and "real art." The performances perplexed Soviet audiences, sometimes inciting public debate and even violence. By 1931, it seems the government had determined that these "literary hooligans" were not doing their part to build socialism.*

Kharms was arrested on December 10, 1931, and interrogated over a period of several months. He was sentenced to three years of labor camp for the crime of "anti-Soviet literary activities." With the help of Maxim Gorky, Kharms made a somewhat successful plea for a decreased sentence and was released for a month in June 1932; he then resumed his sentence in exile from Leningrad for another four months. Upon his return from the provincial city of Kursk in November 1932, Kharms found that Leningrad was becoming progressively more hostile. The OBERIU no longer had a place to perform, nor an audience. All Kharms's hopes of founding a wider alliance of "Left Art" with the artist Kazimir Malevich, the Formalist critics, and other avant-garde literary figures, were dashed against the looming rocks of Socialist Realism.

He continued to write, but only for himself and close friends. The infamous first congress of the Union of Soviet Writers in 1934 proclaimed Socialist Realism as the new ideological model. The stigma of the arrest and increasingly conservative literary tastes made it impossible for Kharms to publish anything but children's poems and stories. By 1937 many of his literary acquaintances had been arrested; some were executed or disappeared in the camps. With the loss of his friends in the publishing world, Kharms was denied even the chance of a small income from his writing for children. On June 1, 1937, Kharms wrote in his journal, "my extermination has begun." A long period of hunger, desperation, and sporadic writing for the desk drawer set in. In spite of nervous disorders and ailing health, Kharms managed to write some of his most impressive works in this period, including the brilliant novella The Old Woman, *his longest prose piece. In 1941, at the onset of the blockade of Leningrad, the not-so-secret police picked up all undesirables in an attempt to minimize the chance of sabotage in the city. Among the undesirables were all those with a previous police record. Thus, Kharms was arrested again in August 1941 and died of hunger on February 2, 1942, in the psychiatric ward at Leningrad Prison No. 1.*

In August of 1994 I was in Moscow, heading to St. Petersburg to research Kharms's manuscripts. At that time, the KGB had changed its name and was trying to do the same with its public image. For that reason KGB officials were under strict orders to be helpful to anyone seeking to view their relatives' records. Thus it was that my grandmother, Elena Bonner, once quite "popular" with this organization, was politely being helped to files concerning herself and her husband, Andrei Sakharov, her mother and father, and various other "enemies of the state." She claimed Kharms was a distant relative of hers and was not asked any questions. We could not photocopy the files, or take pictures, so for the next several days my grandmother and I sat in the reading room of the Moscow KGB from morning to closing, reading the case files into a tape recorder.

The poem that begins "I raised my gaze" was written a month before Kharms's first arrest. (It is impossible to know exactly when the poem was written, as the detective who transcribed the poems jumbled several dates on the page.) This poem and the surrounding diary entries were confiscated from his home, along with "manuscripts, various correspondence, and ten occult-mystical books." They were chosen as an example of Kharms's "anti-Soviet religious attitudes" and entered by the detective into a small "collection" meant for internal use. In addition, the detective may have included these particular journal entries because they were written in "the old orthography," which had since been replaced by Bolshevik orthographic rules. One might even marvel at the astute choices made by the "editor" of this collection, as this poem is representative of Kharms' OBERIU works and artistic philosophy.

The first poem here was called an "excerpt" by the detective who described the work; the longer piece was either lost or never completed. It was included in this collection for its antisocial sentiments and tone of romantic individualism. Similarly, the poem "A Humorous Division of the World in Half," of which only "the second half" was entered by the detective, is an example of Kharms's uncompromising avant-gardism and its formal and linguistic games. Lastly, the story "Blue Notebook No. 10" of 1937 was included in Kharms's desk drawer collection of short stories called Incidences, *and is in many ways a model for his later writings and what has come to be called the "incident" style.*

My translations of the included works are based on the detective's hand-typed version as it appears in the case file. Obviously, some mistakes may have been made in the process of copying the originals, which are probably lost. Particularly suspicious is the inconsistent capitalization, or lack thereof, of the word God, *in the poem "I raised my gaze." Being a deeply (though idiosyncratic) religious person, Kharms would have most likely capitalized* God *throughout the poem, whereas the Soviet detective's motives for using the lowercase are undoubtedly political. On the other hand, Kharms's tendency was to write poems without any capitalization or punctuation whatsoever. To stay on the safe side, in my translation I have closely followed the political police edition, so as not to create further confusion.*

The following excerpt appeared in the file marked:

CASE P-81210, Vol. 2, 1st Edition

Over roads and over deserts
Death walks calling one and all
Through a changing pale-blue sky
Swims the sun.
People crying
People praying
Calling, praying
To the sky,
And the sky keeps silent, shining
All the same people die.
By glorious day
And frightful night
Death is quiet, death is dark
Catching up to those unlucky...
I build a tower on a cliff,
I hide in it.
What do I care of human horrors
what is death to me, what are people.
I live alone in my steeple
I'm smarter than the rest.
The lord of dreams and death
It is my pipe that sings.
I sit at my window and watch all the day,
And sing my songs out loud and brave.
These clumsy people
yet pound on my tower,
while their children weep
and their women howl.
They leave when convinced
there is naught they can do

And loudly they curse me:
you will die too.
Now the elders are gone
and gone all the men
And the children's cry
Is all I hear then.
So drawn out and loud is the wailing I hear,
Let us in, darling, let us in, dear.
And from my window
I yell down to them
Go children go
All of you home
Go children go
You are not needed.

From Kharms's Journal

Saturday, November 14, 1931
The art of silence—that is the gate that leads to heaven.

x x
x

I
raised my gaze higher and higher.
There are the windows of the second story,
There's a mast
There just the sky,
There, heaven
and god in heaven with a face like mine
Yes, I resemble man
and man resembles god
and god resembles the world.
And the tree, the grass, the flower and the leaf
are the beginning of life.
The grass resembles a stone
but the stone crumbles into sand
Sand resembles earth
and into the earth all that is dead seeks to go
The earth lets out a sprout
and gathering moisture
as green clay
lies on the banks of a river
We collect this clay
and sculpt little people
And man was created by god from earth and clay.

Yes, man resembles earth
and earth resembles the world
and the world resembles god.
And I
raise my gaze still higher and higher.
I see that I am created in the image and likeness of God.
And I wander in heaven
And there is no one there
and I shout: But where is god?
And god says to me:
God is I.

Tuesday, November 17, 1931

That which I have written until now, one person has written. If God extends my life I will write again and that which I will write then a different person will write.

Thursday, November 26, 1931

I saw before me a house and that house was at a distance of two hundred and two paces from me.
I came closer and the house now stood at a distance of one hundred and fifty paces from me.
When I came even closer, a man came out of the house and getting down on his knees he began to cry.
"Why are you down on your knees crying?" I asked.
"I am down on my knees crying," he answered, "so that I will not forget the moment when you spoke to me, and so that you will not forget me."

A Humorous Division of the World in Half (Second Half)

The verses lying there before you
and written by my hand
are full of meaningless creation
the laws of all versification
where the beautiful Maria
awoken flies much like a bee...
You were born a meaningspinner
the crooked alleys of your daydreams
and quick nannies' airplanes
when they knock-knocked on the door
along its sides stood open wide
A lantern's light stunk as it died
the sky was sticking to the clouds
The cupboard bowed
and leaning over darling cupboard
in my ear commenced to chide:
Well, go on now, write a log
put some letters side by side
go on pulling on a string
weaving meanings of all things.
Over me Maria's swimming
driving souls out with a switch
quietly big heads and shacks
rest forever in midair
dollies flaming fire maidens
gaze into the hazy heavens
while the plainest simple men
sit below on little benches
First person: This year's winter

will be bitter
the snow will drop
in baskets on our shop
Second Person: *Many nannies will expire*
Birds will trample seeds we've sown
We're in for a bind
though we don't care a bit for nannies
First Person: Have you ever hopped
Second Person: I dented the sky all right
First Person: So I thought you might
Second Person: Yet I've never ever hopped

Both men get up from their little benches and look at each other.
Overhead, simple and light
a flock of peasant birds takes flight
and the flaming maiden dolly
stands at a becoming distance
and in loglike melancholy
the little people promenade
while through the rooms
run fragile barrows
like pebblestones
like firewood they rise

Blue Notebook No. 10

There lived a redheaded man who had no eyes or ears. He didn't have hair either, so he was called a redhead arbitrarily.

He couldn't talk, for he had no mouth. A nose he lacked as well.

He didn't have arms or legs. He had no stomach, no back, no spine, nor did he have any insides. There was nothing to speak of! So, we don't even know what we're talking about.

It's better that we don't talk about him at all.

Date

Quang Bao

Have had problems getting dates since forever
when got one, unsure of outfit.
Lost two vacation days from work to shop for it.
Date shows up ten minutes late
    (must have read that in advice column),
no flowers (disappointment), no wine (unforgivable)

Comes in, takes off at least $750 worth, including shoes
Socks nice, designed by computer probably
Makes difficult to determine size of feet. Possibly 11, overestimate
am optimist, wearing Prada

Open my last bottle of wine
he drinks two glasses before salad tossed.
Touches me but may have been accident
Was reaching for cutlery.

Says, I want to be relaxed tonight.

Good to be relaxed, I say.

As if personality disorder sets in, becomes really shy
Won't stand on same side of kitchen island with me.
When plea made to cut spring onions, he declines,
doesn't want to be misunderstood,
is looking for boyfriend,
wants to go slowly.

How relates to meal, I thought.

He blushes, pours a-no-ther glass.
Am not looking forward to running out of wine this evening.

Meal delicious, thanks Martha. Conversation okay.
Let's go to your couch, he suggests.
Finally, prep work paying off
Feel like on date.
Couch has lovely upholstery but uncomfortable
He sits down on the
op-po-site end of couch.
Am crushed, uncomfortable

As if miracle, puts leg all the way across couch
    nearly touching my pants
Wiggles toes to see if he can make contact.
Lovely, want to marry
Massage my foot if you want to, he says.
Am not into indirect requests

Do you want me to, I ask. Closes his eyes.

Massage foot anyway, hopelessly romantic.
Cannot bear not touching male body parts nearby.
Good massage but very tiring.
    Nearly burned hand while broiling fish earlier.
Am breaking out into sweat. Am careful and slow down.

Make bold move now or return outfit, I think.

I take off his expensive sock. Risky
but nice toes, pedicured and perfect.
Worry about sharing a bank account with person of such.

Kiss my toes, he says, if you want.
Eyes close again. Kiss foot instead.
Decide to let go of leg.

He puts it back down on top of lap and digs heels in.
Pants are now beyond wrinkled.

Guys like you make me love men more, he says.
Not clear of meaning but smile
Don't want to appear unliterary just in case famous quote
You have a fly, he says. Unsure if sexual
but he means, a fly is flying around the room.
He chases it for me—jumps, swats, shrieks at it
Envy fly for all physical effort being exerted on it
Make mental note to pray to be fly when reincarnated.

He sits back down on couch, now wearing one sock and sweaty
Not into locker room fantasy but I endure.
Are you into locker room fantasies, he says.
Yes, I am, I say.

Stands up, takes clothes off, does ten push-ups
Hate men who don't let you do the undressing
All naked now. You do same, please, he says
Makes me take off own clothes
Fold on crease, hang blazer over back of chair,
Suggests I do ten push-ups, but I just ate

It's cold, he says, can you turn up heat?
Very opportunistic, since during dinner
had told him that apartment rent does not include heat.
Am not cold myself but do have more body fat.
Love his goose bumps. Want to count them.

I'll go turn up the heat, he says, as if favor to host
Not mechanical since took too long to accomplish task.
Nice ass though—shape, density, hardness—would like to smack
since not nice to smack face.

We make sex. At times, like fish at dinner
lies there, looks up
Also wiggles a lot and follows orders well.

Nice when naked people cooperate.

His turn-ons: begging, requesting permission beforehand, and always looking into eyes of partner.

My turn-ons: closing eyes, taking without asking, and
opposite of begging.

Ends with a lot of noise. Am very tired suddenly.
Want him to kiss me and be grateful
He does, nicely and sweetly.
Finally, a thought in his head that is same as one in mine.

Nice to feel skin of man. Can't wait for next.
Decide to keep outfit.

Given

Alissa Walser

MY FATHER BREATHES BESIDE ME. WE ARE IN THE HOTEL. TODAY is his birthday, tomorrow is mine. Or maybe it's morning and I've had my birthday, maybe I'm eight by now. I don't know, it's dark. My father does not sleep, just lies there. He'll lie there that way all night long. When he's not asleep, his breath alarms me. Apparently, he thinks that I'm asleep. Then he moves his hands—maybe he has a present for me, hidden under the bedclothes so I can unwrap it as soon as I wake. Or he's trying, just like I do, to find the right position for his hands before he falls asleep. My eyes are closed. He thinks I'm sleeping, but I'm listening to him. I'm afraid he might start to cry. But then he raises himself carefully from the bed, opens the bathroom door and closes it quietly, gently behind him before he turns on the light. He washes his hands. Why can't he just go to sleep?

Today is his sixty-second, tomorrow, my thirty-first, and again my mother is not around. How could she have known her friend would suddenly die like that? Today and tomorrow ought to be days against which my father can, once again, measure the rest of the year. The room is full of flowers and it stinks like a church. My father stands at the brightly lit sideboard. In his house there are no dark corners—his wife sleeps beside him, with me he plays tennis. Sometimes I think he has marked me the way a dog marks a tree. His face and throat both shine with sweat. His hair is a lovely white spit of land in the center of his head extending all the way to his brow. A cell phone protrudes from his jacket pocket and rings continually, turning him into a bell tower. In the next room his new fax machine chirps away—greetings from this or that medical institute. A gift will follow, something he's already got. Probably a classical CD, in which case the recording by the lesser orchestra will soon belong to me.

Ever since I first began to grow breasts, my father has given me money for my birthday. On my thirteenth he told me I looked like the women in Cranach's paintings. I had no idea what he meant by that, but I looked it up. He meant my little bosoms, of which I was ashamed already. Then he pressed a few bills into my palm. I spent the entire year thinking of what I would buy with the money, and then I was fourteen, more crisp bills from Father. I bought a bike. It got stolen. With every birthday the sum of the bills increased. In subsequent years, the money flowed away from me. Six thousand cigarettes, seven hundred cups of coffee, nineteen tubes of lipstick, countless condoms, the collected works of Erich Fromm. At twenty I was designing greeting cards, and Father's gifts sufficed to buy me a computer with graphics capabilities.

This year there are ten large-denomination bills. It is less than the price of a car. I fold the wad in half and jam it in my pocket. Why are you leaving already? asks my father. I don't know, I say.

It's better to arrive in a city on Saturday than Sunday. The people are already starting to glimmer with excitement for the long night ahead. At the station I buy myself a paper with classified ads. In the taxi, under Personals, I find just two listings for women and write the numbers on the back of my hand. This is the way I plunge back into the city where no one is expecting me. In the stairwell I hear my telephone ringing and take two steps at a time till I reach the top floor. Perhaps the gym is the only place you learn anything that matters.

How was the trip? my father asks. I tell him the train was packed, I got a seat in an open car, a young man sat beside me. Nice? he asks. I say I don't know, I had no contact with him, not even eye contact. My father takes a deep breath. He doesn't believe me; he never does when it has to do with men.

What else? he says. I won't starve, I tell him, there's enough in the fridge to last till Monday. And there are ten big bills still undisturbed in my pocket. You could have stayed, you know, then you wouldn't be all alone in the apartment, he says, speaking more of himself than me. So, what are you up to the rest of the day? All right, I tell him, I'll give you some lucky numbers, and I read off a string of digits from the back of my hand: 46925238. Six right in the Saturday drawing, that would be enough to replace me, wouldn't it? My father trusts me. I was fifteen the first time he took me to the casino. Too young to play, they said at the door after checking my ID. I felt accused. But they let me in to bring him good luck, and I hovered behind him on the tips of my toes, whispering numbers in his ear till I could no longer stand straight. Whenever he lost a lot, he'd leave the building in a hurry. Then the car wouldn't start, then every light was red. Papa gunned it, Papa slammed the breaks, Papa gunned it again. I laid my head down on the backseat, looked at the stars, and prayed to the mother of God, in whom I did not believe. Branches, lights, branches. I stayed down. I didn't want to die sitting up.

My father takes down the numbers I give him and we hang up. Later I call the first of the two listings. A guy answers. Describe yourself, I say. I mean it. He tells me about each of his features, and pretty quickly I know I don't want to see him. Then I call the other one. A guy answers. I can hear the chirpings of a lovebird in the background. Big, he says, dark, twenty-three, from the South. How much, I say. How much have you got? And already I know I love him. Finally someone I can talk to. Or just say nothing. If he tries to give me advice, I'll send him away. He'll have to take me as I come, and I will do with him what I like. This boy will show me his chest and ask me to show him mine. With this boy I will overcome the evening, the day of rest, possibly even the March weather.

My father calls in the evening. He just has to breathe and I know who it is. Stop your breathing, I say. What have you been up to, he says. He always wants to know that. He always wants to know where I've been, who was with me, what we did, and then what. The livelier I sound, the harder he presses. What would he say if he ran out of questions? But he won't. And there's still the entire stockpile of questions he's never asked me: Who loves you, how much is he worth, who believes in you, who is disappointed, who hangs onto your every word, who pays for you, how rich is he, who pulls us both up out of our own shit, what have you done, are you like me, why are you like me, who's going to save us now, how is your cunt, is it worth it, does it make you good money, why don't you have children, where is your Messiah now? I want to give him some answer that forbids all further questions.

I'm glad I came yesterday, I say. I didn't have any plans, but with all that money in my pocket, it isn't half as bad. My father is disturbed that I only have eight of the bills remaining. No, I wasn't gambling, I tell him, I bought myself a boy. And I keep on speaking without any pause so my father doesn't have a chance to ask me about his face. It was an incomplete face, I thought. That boy will have to go through all sorts of things before his face is finished. I could, for example, tell my father it was an Italian face, but he'd rather hear it was the face of someone who's climbed over the Wall, a former East German. Then my father would be able to applaud his courage, applaud the little bit of historical reality, the extra credit that life would have given him, just like that, without the boy's ever having to do anything about it. I say only that his hair was dark, black but not blue-black, uncombed. I remind my father of how, when I would come out of the bath, he used to compare me to a freshly peeled fruit. That was the kind of boy it was, I tell him, and ask if he understands. No, he says. Fax him to me.

My father's breathing is drowned out by the sound of the opening door, as he steps out into the garden. Maybe he's just out getting some air. He loves to walk around with his cell phone. Even on a Sunday morning at an hour when no one would call, he's always got the phone with him. The wife and daughter are still asleep, and he moves about the lawn in his pajamas, picking up sticks that have made their way onto his lawn from the forest during the night. I see something you don't see, he says. Know what it is? The forest. The forest is darker than the night. Today the sky was blinding gray. Yesterday I saw a young woman pushing a stroller, she used to go to school with you, you sat right next to her. We're not in contact, I tell him. Your generation, he says. What do all the other people your age do with themselves? I don't know what you mean, I say. Have babies. Make excuses. Wear white dresses. Travel. And you go out and buy yourself a man, he says suddenly. Just this once, I say. Tell me about it. He lights a cigarette.

Just before twilight, we went out to a restaurant. That's what I wanted to do, and I was in charge. It's a place I'd never go to by myself, with heavy beer-hall tables. My father interrupts: Was the food good, at least? He sounds like he's praying for a painless death. He has no idea how unimportant the food was. Whenever I go out to eat with him, he orders me some kind of colorful special plate, something with a litle bit of everything on it, too playful for grownups, too serious for children. Or bivalves, which he'd never order for himself. He wants me to eat his oysters for him.

I sat there in front of a glass of water, I tell him. The boy had a hunk of meat, then a coffee, then another coffee. It wasn't like it had been on the phone. He seemed to know exactly what he wanted. Astounding, the control he had over his features. A smile appeared abruptly on his lips, then, just as suddenly, it vanished. When his plate was empty, he asked me what I wanted. It was clear to me, I tell my father, that he was already thinking about the end. I didn't want to discuss that. I didn't want to make anything hard and fast. My father sucks his cigarette like a kid making fish faces. I can't stand his cigarettes and neither can my mother. We're not wasps, you know, she tells him, when he's filled the entire room with smoke. The boy stroked me behind the ear and whispered something to me. He thought I was being shy. We weren't talking much after that, which I didn't like. There was no reason for silence. So I told him to tell a story. I would have liked him to tell me a deep-sea-fishing tale about creatures living in places that men have never been. He was fiddling with the tassels on his scarf, which hung around his neck like a boxer's towel. As I rubbed the fabric between my fingers, he started to talk about money. He wanted to start a company that sold some health-promoting product. Suddenly I saw his desperation, I told my father, and considered whether I wouldn't rather pass the afternoon at the movies. Can you imagine laying your hands on a desperate person? I asked. You've done it before, said my father, my God, so quietly I could barely hear him. My father loathes nothing more than unhappiness; he can hardly even stand to look at someone who's leading a life he wouldn't want. He wants heroes for me, stars of the silver screen. We've never been to a movie theater together. Films made after 1958 don't interest him at all—that's supposedly the year that Doris Day turned thirty. Sometimes we watch old Hollywood pictures on television. First, my father waits for the stars to appear, then he waits for the ending. Between these high points, he sits there staring at the screen as if he were dead. Last week we almost came to blows. Judy Garland was in the cast, and he was waiting for her. A couple of young singers had already come on, and more than once he'd called out, That's her! Each time I told him I thought otherwise, his fury mounted. Then she appeared and sang her number. She looks a little like you, my father said. It doesn't matter who it is, my father always sees a resemblence between me and the stars. The last time it was Loren, before that Bergman. He'll say Liz Taylor if there's nothing on the TV at the moment. Marilyn's the only one he never compares me to. She's the Holy Virgin to him, and there's only one of those.

From the noises I'm hearing, the light creaking of the parquet floor, he's gone into the living room. Where's the drawing, he says. I watch my sketch disappear into the slot of my fax machine, his old one. I hear the wine falling into his glass. I give my father time to take that first long gulp, it beeps, then his machine prints my drawing on a sheet of paper.

Aha, says my father. Then a moment of silence, and then he asks, What is that? Forget about it, I say, and keep telling him what happened. I'm here just for you, the boy told me. He asked me to trust him. I'm sure it would have been better for him if I'd told him a little about myself, but I said nothing. He prattled on about money and when, for the first time, his smile failed him, I did what I always do—comforted him. He was supposed to be there, happily, for me. Tell me something, interrupted my father, you wanted him? Patience, I said. After he ate, there seemed to be no place to go. I could tell he wanted his money, but the main event was still to come. I didn't feel like paying for a hotel, and I didn't want him at my place. He suggested his apartment, but I didn't want to meet the lovebird either. I suggested we wait till it was dark outside. In the dark I was sure there would be a place. I'll pay you for every minute, I told him. I saw he wanted his money up front, but what had he done for me so far? Looked at me like I was pretty, stroked my nose with his index finger and the place behind my ear. That was all just the buildup to the day's decisive moment.

From my father, nothing. Not a breath. I ask if he's still on the line. Yes, he says, go on. He listens to me with complete attention. Perhaps if he finds the whole thing remarkable enough, he'll give a lecture on it at his next conference. Then I'll have to repeat it for him over and over. When he likes a story, he always wants to hear it a hundred times and usually complains that I play down the good parts. But perhaps, this time, he won't say anything at all, and I'll be overwhelmed with pity. I dread that more than his wrath. All this time, my father's pacing. His footsteps echo, and I can hear him going upstairs. Upstairs in the bedrooms, the connection is bad, and it always sounds like a snowstorm is raging outside. Too early to go to bed, isn't it? I ask. He tells me he wants to be in my room, he thinks it will be easier to understand me from there. I know your tricks, I say. What's he doing in my room? But more important is how I bring the story to a close. I must recall it exactly. It seemed we walked through the city a long time. The boy told me I was a terrific person, the kind he'd always wanted to be with. My father coughs a little and I hear him wash down the cough with wine. The boy tried to kiss me, I tell him, but I wouldn't let him. I do not tell my father I was afraid. I know just what he'd say to that: The one who pays should not be afraid. But the boy might have changed his mind at any moment and walked away. I got the idea that we should do it in the entryway of a building, but the doors were locked. I rang a bell, and someone stuck his head out the window, but he wouldn't let us in. Even the nooks of the old city wall, the shelter of which I'm familiar with, suddenly weren't deep enough. I hope you were warmly dressed, says my father. Yes, I tell him, the coat. And what else, underneath, he wants to know. I tell him. The boy was waiting for me to give him some word, but I said nothing for fear I'd say something wrong.

At the park he stopped and shook his head. He led me over to where he'd left his car. Someday, he said, as he opened the door, I'll have a helicopter. We got in the car. It was just like any other car. He sat beside me, in the driver's seat. Probably my father also wonders why the boy didn't open the back doors.

It was too dark to see, I tell him. I knew the boy was waiting for a cue. I couldn't get this sentence out of my head: I want your secret meat. I said it so quietly he didn't understand. My father says nothing. I hear him breathing. I have never thought of my father's body as old. When I was a child, I wanted to be like him. I wanted to smell like him, of liquor and cigarettes at night and in the morning, when I visited him in bed, like sweat and sleep. He was larger than I, more shapeless, plumper. Even so, I wanted to be grown. When I asked him to come down to me, to the floor, he groaned. But that did not make him seem fragile. I wasn't even repulsed by the scales of his psoriasis—at most by the ointments he used to treat it. Now his breathing sounds different than usual, and there is a new silence between us. Maybe his breathing will grow heavier and heavier from this point on, until it is prematurely like that of an old man. I must tell him not to spend so much time with people who bring him close to death. The boy, I tell him, he took my hand. I gave my hand to him, and he used it to stroke his thigh. In the warm crease where the thigh meets the sex, he left my hand to its own devices, and the back of my hand brushed up against his balls. I rubbed the loose skin of his scrotum between my fingers. I think my father is waiting for the climax, but I would never give that to him. I tell him of the color of the skin that I never actually saw. I say it was darker than elsewhere. The boy groped for the same place on me. Then, with one motion, the way you would withdraw your hand from someone else's pocket, we pulled back our hands to ourselves. I paid what he asked, got out of the car, headed home. Call me anytime, he called, before I slammed the door. I'm always here for you. And now I just got home, I tell my father. I'm opening up the other gifts. Chanel No. 19 and Mozart's Concerto No. 3 in G Major, performed by the Bamburg Symphony—given. Later I'll make some pasta and a sauce to go with it, tomatoes and something green. Tomorrow is Monday, and you know what I do on Mondays.

My father did not respond again. I still don't know why. Hello, I said. I see something you don't see—nothing. There was just a slight change in the background noise in the receiver, a gnawing at the white noise. My father was just lying there. Then I heard a rustling of the bedclothes. Perhaps he was trying to find the right position for his hands before he fell asleep. I was afraid he might start to cry. I was afraid he might flail about. I wanted only to be silent, completely silent, completely gentle, as gentle as the closing of the door to a child's room when at last it is quiet inside. I hung up the phone.

Translated from the German by Elizabeth Gaffney

"Oh, for a diet of toasted cheese and the company of those he found amusing."
(Dannatt, page 87)

Excuse

Rick Snyder

Please pardon me
for being late.
I had intended to arrive
by 8:30,
but after listening
to "Baby Hold on to Me"
I left the castle,
and we all went fishing
in Shanklin Pond.
Mike caught a trout
the size of his leg,
and we beat it
mercilessly,
using our aluminum bats
until it was
pulp and bone,
a poultice we applied
to the wounds
we incurred earlier,
when holding off
the filthy Amish.
Thank you,
Rick Snyder

Pop Poem '98

Rick Snyder

My soup will expire
in Mar 00
DO NOT ADD WATER
Andy's flesh already
swoop swoops the soup
is heating I'm eating
it even now my split
pea spit tastes foul
from the broth that
used to be chicken
slickensides fold-axe
are how I translate
the act of soup produced
by can opener left
for me bereft
of a girlfriend

To You, My Reader

Mark Gonzales

THE KING LOVED HIS GARDEN. HE LOVED WATERING THE PLANTS. The king had to stop watering when a tiny bug entered his nasal passage. Sniffing and blowing, the king tried desperately to rid himself of the little insect, but it seemed impossible. The king fell over and died there in his garden.

The king's venomous spirit leapt from his body and into the soil. "Now whatever sprouts from the ground is of evil origin," the townspeople declared. So, many years went by and the people went without a king and only ate what was not of the earth, and their diets were unbalanced and lopsided until a solo man descended upon the town. His clothing was worn out and his hair was matted and woolly. His name was of no importance. He simply knew all without being told. This frightened the people and they did not know what to make of the strange foreigner. The foreigner asked, "Have you people had a king?"

"Yes," the people replied.

"And did you not treasure what he treasured?"

Everyone was silent, because just days before the king's death the people passed him off as an unfit king, a king who only liked to see things grow, especially in his garden. The people wanted a king who would take down other thrones and dominate new territory. So not one single sound was heard. The foreigner picked up a handful of soil.

"The king's death has enriched the soil. Please forgive yourselves for not believing in what your king believed in. The ground is good ground; the soil is rich. It will feed those who are hungry."

The people screamed insults to the foreigner. Soon, with angry remarks, stones flew.

The people's bodies began to look irregular. Their diets were not right. In fact, many had died. Soon the people got desperate, but still they refused to eat from the earth. It was always when they were desperate that someone would arrive. This time the foreigner came from the sea in a ship that was black. This new messenger was in nice clean clothes and he was accompanied by several other men who stood close beside him. The new messenger people liked. He emerged from the sea and not the earth. He was nicely groomed and master of a group of strong-looking men. The new king told the people, "You are all ugly."

"Yes," the people said. "We are ugly. We don't eat from the earth."

The man from the big black ship, the new king, said, "Please, you must eat from the earth."

The people saw the new king's strength and power over so many strong-looking men and believed whatever he said was right. The people then ate from the earth. Soon after, they all took notice that the new king who had come from the sea was not eating from the earth. They asked, "Why do you not eat from the earth?"

The king said, "Don't be fooled by me. I eat from the earth where I come from."

The people with the food in their tummies knew they had been fooled. The king bade the dying people farewell as he and his men returned to the big black ship to sail for home.

The Final Man

Susan Perry

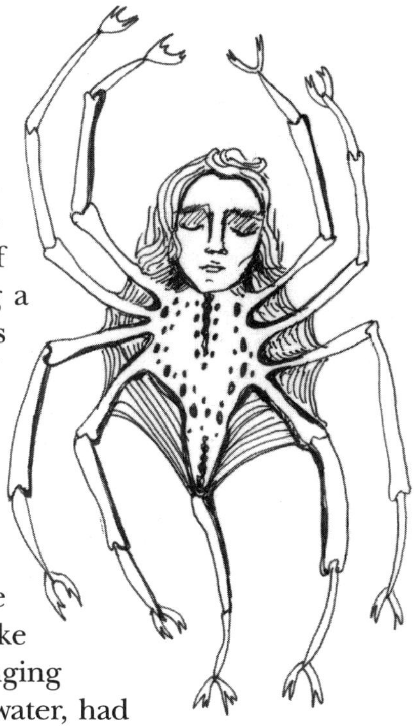

ON APRIL 13, 1998, WHEN DIVERS PULLED the body of forty-eight-year-old Frederick Lenz from Conscience Bay, off his shoreline estate in the affluent community of Old Field, Long Island, he was wearing a Versace suit, black tie, overcoat, dress shoes, and the worn cloth dog collar of his recently deceased Scottish terrier, Vayu, which had an outdated rabies vaccination tag attached. Dental records were needed to identify him. His desiccated, rigor-mortised form was made all the more disturbing by the fact that a slew of half-foot-long spiderlike sand crabs, the only marine life scavenging the bottom of the bay in forty-degree water, had shredded the skin of his face with their pincer-like claws.

Frederick Lenz was a spiritual guru–cum–cult leader for two decades. He promised his followers "the short track to enlightenment," in which high-end materialism replaced what he called the "begging bowl" mentality of traditional Buddhism. According to his students, no one has yet accurately described the profound experience of loving Lenz, known as Rama, also referred to as Buddha, the Chief, the Boss, and the Man, an enlightened being incarnated in this lifetime as a gangly, six-foot-three, androgynous-featured, acne-scarred, *Frampton Comes Alive*–hairstyled regular Joe.

Illustrations by Bettina Hubby

He claimed that his previous incarnations included a Tibetan lama, a temple elder in Atlantis, and a teacher of the occult in ancient Egypt. And in the months preceding his death, Lenz repeatedly stated that this was his last incarnation. He'd had enough of this hell world, thousands of lifetimes in fact. During his final seminars he often spoke of his pain, how his suffering had become unbearable. His dog had recently died. He was reduced to wearing bullet-proof clothing because of his vigilant detractors. And he would never achieve his ultimate dream, to buy an island in the South Pacific—his refuge from the onslaught of media scrutiny, of which he said, "I feel like a character in a Kafka novel. I am continually accused by the spurious press of things I have not done."

He believed his students were trying to kill him with their occult powers. They were making his skin chafe a bruised red and his dyed-blond locks fall out. He'd developed an addiction to Valium, drank exorbitant quantities of tequila, had liver problems and

tinnitus, and was rumored to have had a stroke; he continually attributed his bad health to his followers. He told them that they were "in the soup," which meant they had been assailed by evil spiderlike entities, lower occult forces that had invaded their psyches, driving them insane. During his seminars he gave a play-by-play of these vexing creatures sticking their spindly legs into the ears of his oblivious students. He had developed a terror of spiders, and on several occasions when he saw one traversing a wall he scurried off, screaming out in his high-pitched voice, which has been compared to that of fitness missionary Richard Simmons, for someone to kill the little devil. He called his students "pathetic slime buckets" and raised their "tuition" with each perceived psychic assault against him. Still, he was said to glow bright like a Christmas angel, the gold luminosity of his aura sometimes yielding rainbows. Sometimes he metamorphosed into an Oriental man who levitated two feet off the ground with a fire torch for a hand. To some, he was the Almighty himself. To many, he was the funniest man alive. His comedy routines were endearingly referred to by his devotees as his "Rodney Dangerfield." He challenged his disciples to hot-sauce-chugging contests, and liked to give monologues on the movies that inspired him most, including *A Nightmare on Elm Street, Part I* and *Part III.* And when he condemned them to cancer and AIDS, his voice turned from the occasional "Hey, sport, sending on happy thoughts" cheery goodwill to a vituperative snarl. If they did not stop attacking him, he said, an agonizing fifty-thousand-lifetime cruise through the hell worlds was what they had to look forward to. And then, after making clear that his omnipotence had rigged him with a clear bird's-eye view into their depraved thoughts, into their nefarious desires to fuck with him, he disappeared.

The Suffolk County Medical Examiner's Office ruled Lenz's death a suicide by drowning. The intended means of suicide was drug overdose, according to Brinn Lacey, the thirty-eight-year-old ex-model and student of Lenz's who was found by police at 2 A.M. in the upstairs bedroom of his secluded, heavily secured pagoda-style mansion with a note she'd written by her side: "We all tried to go to the other woorld last night, and only Rama made it. Please help us make it to the other woorld." Lacey said she had swallowed fifty Valium to Lenz's one hundred and fifty, after she and Lenz had drugged their Scottish terriers' kibble with phenobarbital.

Lacey led them to the meticulously kept two-acre backyard, past the hot tub, the five-foot-tall Buddhist temple sculptures, the American flags, the beds of blooming tulips and rhododendrons, past the security cameras and gates, down a steep flight of stairs to the floating pier. At the end of the pier a railing was broken and a piece of rope hung limply. Lacey said that the bruises on her face and body were the result of attempting to pull Lenz from the bay after he plummetted in. She managed to pull herself and the dogs from the water and upstairs, where she proceeded to ingest forty-five phenobarbital and a half bottle of rum, and waited to die while staring at a photograph of Lenz and his dead dog, Vayu. Lacey, referred to by Lenz as Savitri (a Hindu word meaning *savior*), had for many years been known as Lenz's favorite disciple. In 1982, Lacey, a blonde-haired, blue-eyed Bostonian who'd on one occasion graced the pages of *Vogue,* was living in Los Angeles with a boyfriend who regularly beat her when, on a checkout line, a copy of *Self-Discovery,* a free promotional newspaper Lenz published, caught her eye. "Picking up that paper felt like grabbing a hand that just at the last minute reached out to save me from falling off a high cliff," she told one magazine. She saw Lenz's photograph on the back page. "I tell you, I dug this guy in the picture so much, I could hardly stand it. How brazen, how outlandish, how glorious." Throughout the eighties, Lacey went from being Lenz's student and lover to housekeeper, and after she was fired and replaced by another Lenz devotee, she waited for his phone call for more than half a decade.

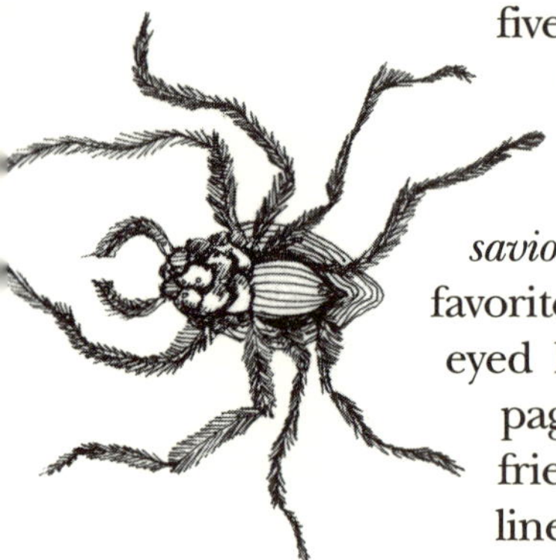

When he finally called in early 1997, he told her that every one of his students wanted to kill him and that it was only her, Savitri, that he trusted. Then he laid out the plan of his suicide. Lacey asked if he would allow her to die along with him. He consented and said that the dogs must die too, and that Padme, Lacey's dog, was a pure spirit who would lead their way to a higher spiritual plane. For a week, they meditated, took long walks in the woods and drives into Southampton. Lacey massaged Lenz's feet for hours at a time, secretly hoping that he would back out of the suicide, that in fact he was only testing her devotion to him. No matter what his course of action, however, she was determined not to fail him. Jointly, they decided that the appropriate place to do it was the water. Although neither liked the cold, the idea of being carried out to sea seemed heroic. After stumbling down the steps to the bay with the dogs, the leashes tightly wrapped around their wrists, Lacey remembers little else. The toxicologists who measured the quantity of barbiturates in her blood two days later were astounded that she had survived. A week after admittance to the psychiatric ward, Lacey was released, whereupon she recalled her final image of Lenz, his jacket a black bubble slowly gliding across the surface of the water, his face to the bottom of the bay, and then disappearing.

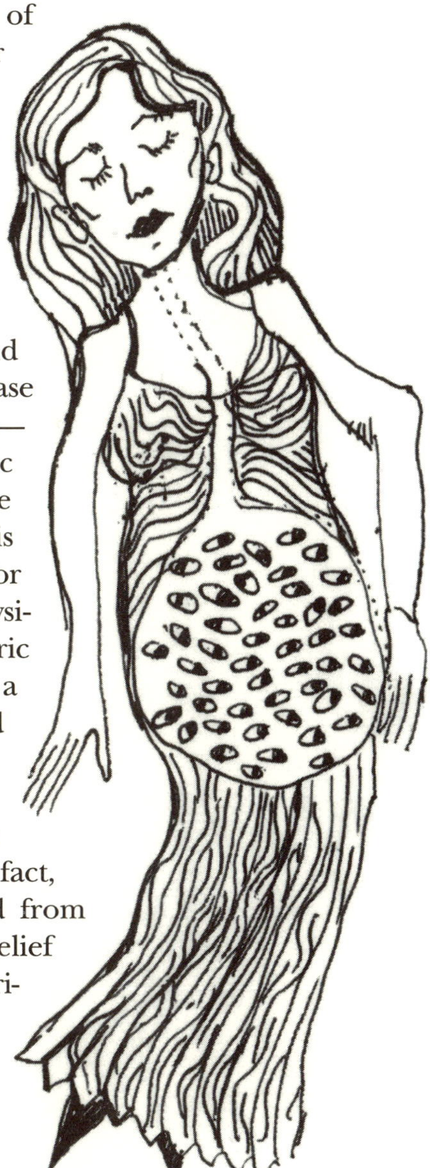

This time, however, it was not the kind of miracle act Lenz was inclined to showcase on- stage in classic Siegfried and Roy style—suddenly vanishing, awash in majestic light, reappearing moments later to the astonished silence of his audience. This time was his final farewell. Nonetheless, for many of his followers the loss of Lenz physically was of little consequence. His auric presence continued to be perceived as a source of Christlike energy; his death and the bizarre circumstances of it were seen as another in a series of mysterious life lessons, a sad but highly significant gift from their devoted teacher. And yes, in fact, another awe-inspiring magic trick pulled from the hat, because it was their deep-rooted belief that the lesson and the magic were inextricably bound, despite how difficult it is to pinpoint exactly what the lesson was.

Lenz was born in San Diego and grew up in Stamford, Connecticut. He recalled spending the better part of his childhood wandering around his parents' parties, acting as spiritual guide to the many disillusioned guests who relied on him for his psychic gifts. According to Lenz, as a child his extrasensory abilities set him apart from others, creating an interminable loneliness. When Lenz was five his parents got divorced. His mother subsequently turned to booze and LSD—both of which she readily parceled out to her teenage son. An astrologer by trade, Mrs. Lenz's parting words of advice to her son moments before she died, when Lenz was a teenager, was to watch the movie *M*A*S*H*. Lenz's father, the mayor of Stamford during the seventies, frequently beat him, according to Lenz, but these episodes only increased his single-minded determination to live up to what he saw as his enlightened birthright.

In high school Lenz liked to preach, instruct people, and be the center of attention. Often tripping on LSD, he still managed to make converts to whatever spiritual or philosophical practice he was espousing at the time. In 1973, Lenz received a B.A. from Connecticut College. Five years later, he earned a Ph.D. in English literature from the State University of New York at Stony Brook, where he did his doctoral dissertation on "The Evolution of Matter and Spirit in the Poetry of Theodore Roethke."

Busted for selling pot while living in San Francisco, Lenz spent a year at a work camp and then moved back to Connecticut, where he apprenticed himself to the famed Hindu guru and physical fitness cultist Sri Chinmoy. Chinmoy claimed to possess supernatural powers—students included luminaries such as Carlos Santana and John McLaughlin. Lenz worked as a teacher at Chinmoy's ashram in Jamaica, Queens, where he excelled as a recruiter. However, when the guru learned of Lenz's many sexual exploits with female followers, he exiled Lenz to San Diego to work in a Laundromat in an effort to "teach him humility."

Instead, in 1979, Lenz broke from Chinmoy and became a guru in his own right. He first called himself Atmananda, derived from the Hindu word *Atman,* defined as "The supreme and universal soul, from which all souls arise." Lenz's group, named

Lakshima, after the Hindu goddess of beauty and prosperity, focused primarily on the enlightenment of women. Advertisements for Lakshima included posters of a barely-clad blonde in the lotus position atop a red Porsche. Lenz permitted no one over the age of twenty-nine into the group. He moved with his core of followers, a number fast rising toward five-hundred, from San Diego to Los Angeles to Boston to San Francisco, and then to Virginia, the tuition incrementally rising from $5 per seminar to $2,500.

By 1985, Lenz had conferred upon himself the title *Rama,* another Hindu term, meaning the three incarnations of Vishnu, one of the chief deities worshiped as a hero. Lenz's controversial brand of spirituality was fashioned on his interpretations of Hinduism, Zen, Tantric Buddhism, the philosophy of Carlos Castaneda, and Lenz's own ethos, which was akin to, and continually evolving toward, the blossoming have-it-all Reaganomics of the time. "At first, he mostly talked about the nature of Buddha, Nirvana, and a lot about enlightenment," says Steve Kaplan, a student of Lenz's for fifteen years who joined the group in 1982. "Sometimes he talked about computer programming, or Shakespeare, or he did what he called his Johnny Carson routines. 'We gotta give the people what they came for,' he'd say. Usually the focus was on spirituality though, the Bhagavad Gita and the Tibetan Book of the Dead. Lenz had an extremely sharp intellect. And there was this energy and light coming from him. I thought I'd found the real thing. But then he got into weird shit. He was taking Percodan all day long. He'd give them to me and say, 'It's a bad day, lots of bad energy.' He had us read Stephen King's book *It* twice—twelve hundred pages about this spidery entity taking over. He'd say, 'Stevie's catching something here. He's not even conscious he's doing it, but he's tapping into something big.'"

Kaplan recalls, "It was around this time that Lenz had a couple of meetings devoted to Sri Chinmoy where he said that Chinmoy was really a big spider inside what looked like Chinmoy's body, and that he was responsible for everything wrong in his students' lives. If they couldn't get a job, it was Chinmoy. If they didn't feel like getting out of bed in the morning, it was Chinmoy. 'But don't worry about it,' he said. 'I'm going to make him sorry he was ever born. I'm going to destroy his body on a psychic level.'" During this time, Lenz maintained that no one was to be trusted, particularly longstanding members of his group whose lower occult abilities, he said, were acutely honed. In Lenz's seminar titled "Psychic Self-Defense" he said, "Just like the vampire in the old movies can drain blood from his victims, it's possible to tap into people's life energy. The more you trust a person the greater the possibility of manipulation. They will psychically inject their fears into you. The only way to protect yourself is by learning to become inaccessible." Lenz's idea of inaccessibility included no shaking of hands, no kissing on the cheek, no touching of any kind, except during sex, when vital life forces could still be siphoned off, he said, but it was worth the risk. Lenz told his students to unlist their telephone numbers, to get post-office boxes, and to cut all communication with family and friends. However, he cautioned that during sleep, on a "dream plane," it was even harder to protect yourself from "psychic stalking." "If you wake up feeling not refreshed," Lenz cautioned, "that means that you got attacked by someone during your sleep." To be killed on a dream plane was not an uncommon occurrence; a knife in the heart was the most likely way to go. He advised his followers to set their alarm clocks to ring every hour, jolting them back into reality, or to refrain from sleeping much at all. If these strategies were ineffective, he suggested moving to another country. "He had everyone paranoid. It was horrible to watch and it just kept getting worse," Kaplan says. "He'd walk around the seminar room, a group of four hundred followers sitting there, and he'd accuse each of us of trying to kill him. He drummed it into us for so long that at a certain point people would just

stand up and admit it."

Teri Corasel was living in Arizona in 1984 when she heard a radio advertisement for Lenz's upcoming seminar "Why More Women Don't Attain Enlightenment" at the Scottsdale Hilton. At twenty-six, Teri was lonely and careerless and yearning for a sense of community. She immediately liked Lenz. He was tall, and she'd always been attracted to tall men. Also, she found him to be extremely funny. He wore a bright red tennis outfit and filled the auditorium with hundreds of furry, multicolored hand-puppets called Blisses. Lenz spoke as if in a trance, intermittently breaking out in giggles. But Teri was most struck by how genuinely concerned Lenz seemed for the spiritual growth of women. He compelled the five hundred inhabitants in the room to meditate for four straight hours without a break. And though Teri was hungry and tired, she says she transcended to a beatific state of relaxation, the likes of which she'd never experienced before. She remembers the salmon-colored curtains on the stage behind Lenz wavering in a vaporous stream, like gasoline fumes cascading with plumes of air on a hot day. She wondered if she was hallucinating. She didn't care. Whatever was happening felt great. Having just broken up with her boyfriend, and feeling restless for a life change, Teri moved to Boston, where Lenz was conducting seminars.

During seminars, Lenz emphasized the importance of remaining celibate. He was strongly opposed to marriage and children, seeing these commitments as an intrinsic drain for those on a spiritual quest; his disciples believed that Lenz's sexual abstinence was a sign of his metaphysical and moral perfection. However, during seminar breaks, Teri, a pretty blonde, remembers, "He was looking me up and down, walking in circles around me, checking me out. I thought this was odd. But then I thought that he was looking into my soul, into all my past lives. Finally, he approached me and said, 'You're a good person, Teri. I'd like to get together with you.' Teri said that Lenz treated her courteously, unlike his dealings with his other female students. "He'd have a woman stand up in front of everyone and he'd say, 'Now tell everyone how horrible you really are,' and she'd say, 'I'm horrible. I wish some people would get sick and die. I wish you would die.' And they'd look at him like, 'Am I saying it right? Is that what I'm feeling?' He said he loved everyone, that we were all good people, and in the next second he could call us slime buckets." Lenz told Teri that one day she too might start jabbing psychic spears into the stomachs of her fellow students, but that she'd not been around long enough to propagate such evil occultism.

The first time Teri visited Lenz at his home he introduced her to his Scottish terriers and led her on an accelerated tour that concluded in his bedroom. He excused himself to the bathroom and returned wearing only his tight white briefs and carrying a bottle of lotion. Teri was not suspicious. She thought, "He's the Buddha. He probably only wears clothes so as not to embarrass people." When he sat on the bed and asked her to massage his back, she felt enormously honored. She assumed he only allowed the purest of souls to touch him. She recounts, "I'm putting the lotion on his back and he asks, 'Can you feel the energy running through me?' And I said, 'Sorry, but no.' He said, 'Okay, no problem. Can you get my legs now?' Then he flipped onto his back and somehow his underwear was off. He took my hands and laid them on his groin. And I thought, 'What does he want me to do?' It didn't enter my mind that sex was where he was leading. I didn't see him as human. Finally, he pushed me down so I was touching him with my mouth. I almost started crying. I was really confused."

Over the course of the next five years Teri received a dozen calls from Lenz in the middle of the night inviting her to his Long Island mansion. "The last five times he treated me like a hooker. 'Go take a shower and get in bed. I'll meet you there. I know what you want,'" Teri remembers him saying. Teri soon came to learn of the two dozen female students having sex with Lenz who were referred to, herself included in this company, as the Witches. One evening he sat them in a circle and told them that he was having sex with all of them because they were in the midst of supremely difficult times and needed extra support.

Of this select group of women, Lenz took LSD with those who were willing, and instructed the others to take what he told them was Benadryl—to protect them from his cold. Several recalled that this purported over-the-counter medication caused them to hallucinate wildly, or else to fall into a dreamlike slumber before blacking out. Sometimes, when he emerged from the bathroom in his underwear he'd be holding a tube of lubricant, other times he brandished a pistol that he would place on the bedside table. Many recalled the rifle that he kept under his pillow. At first, he courted them with extreme generosity—wining and dining them, taking them to Europe on his Learjet, purchasing gifts of clothes and jewelry, spending upwards of $20,000 over the course of a few hours. Always, he said that they had been lovers during a past life in Egypt. Sex was a favor he was doing for them; this spilling over of his liquid enlightenment (sperm) was a means to expand their consciousness, and nothing that he enjoyed. In the postcoital quiet they dutifully thanked him, usually just as he was sticking a video into the VCR, perhaps *Terminator* or *Groundhog Day*, two of his favorites, which he watched dozens of times. And for those who got pregnant, he always paid for the abortions. Occasionally, he talked about the "Zen of cleaning the toilet bowl" and introduced those game for the task to his upstairs bathroom. Some were privy to his episodic "demon-cleaning sprees." Donning a yellow rain slicker and American Indian jewelry, he'd cautiously descend the stairs to his basement and swing a broom around, whacking at the walls, kicking and karate-chopping the air in a warriorlike mission to destroy the evil arachnids skulking invisibly in the shadows, besieging him in his dreams.

The last time Teri rendezvoused with Lenz, she drove sixteen hours from Virginia to his rented town house in Vermont. For dinner, he handed her a bag of M&M's and a can of Jolt cola. After having sex, Teri says, "He told me to get out. He said I was bringing bad vibrations into his house, that I was just a bitch like all the others." While trying to muffle her sobs on the way to the car, she paused when she heard Lenz's trademark hand clapping and heavy moaning—his idea of an exorcism for particularly injurious energy. On the long drive home Teri wept the entire way, feeling diseased and worthless. From that point on, at seminars, Lenz no longer acknowledged her, and she recalls that when the new shipload of "young blood" came in she knew that he would be personally tour-guiding many of them to his bedroom, and it hurt.

In the mid-eighties, Lenz introduced fellow students Steve Kaplan, a musician and composer who had done the scores for *Jeopardy* and *Terms of Endearment,* to Andy West, the bass player from the Dixie Dregs, and Joaquin Lievano, who had played with Jean-Luc Ponté. At Lenz's behest they formed a band, Zazen (at one time called Nirvana). When they got signed with Miramar Records instead of Sony, Lenz's first choice, Kaplan says that Lenz accused him of psychically sabotaging his dreams of commercial success. In an attempt to get more exposure for Zazen, Lenz produced and starred in a racy music video for the song "What is Dancing?" For the video, a bevy of Playboy Bunnies danced in stark contrast to Lenz, who labored considerably with his hip gyrations. The video was never released. During that time, Lenz rented Sting's Malibu beach house for $25,000 a month in order, he said, "to tap his consciousness and become successful in the music business."

In many ways, Lenz's life was fast becoming the baby-boomer dream gone mad. The material guru clamored for fame and celebrity while his inner resources seemed to be quickly eroding, leaving him depressed and largely delusional. In the early nineties, he sent several of his "Witches" to Redmond, Washington. They were instructed to sleep with Bill Gates, and steal his source code. During seminars, he said he would bring Microsoft down, that he would become the next Bill Gates. But this grand plan had to be dropped, Lenz said, due to the Cult Awareness Network's spying on him. (C.A.N. is the watchdog group that investigated the Scientologists, eventually becoming a Scientologist front itself). Lenz claimed to be a computer architect who designed systems, though it was common knowledge that he was illiterate in programming languages. Nonetheless, he was CEO of ten privately held high-tech companies that employed many of his followers, who signed contracts granting Lenz 50 percent of their earnings. "You know I am power," he said to Steve Kaplan months before his suicide. "In order to work with you I have to empower you."

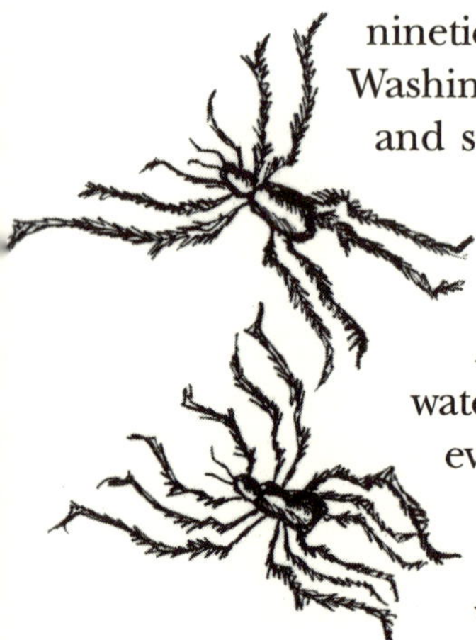

In 1988, a half dozen women went public with denunciations of Lenz in the *San Francisco Chronicle*, *L.A. Weekly*, and other publications. The torrent of negative publicity threw him into a severe depression. He announced that he was soon going to renounce his role as spiritual guru. "I'm willing to change your diapers and clean up your shit for a couple of years," Lenz told his followers, "but after a while you're going to be toilet trained and you're going to dress yourself. What the teacher does is say, 'Okay, sucker, I've pulled the karma for you. I've taken your bad energy into my body. Now you'll learn how unpleasant it is when someone is not always cleaning up your messes.'" Although month after month, Lenz threatened to desert his students, his seminars continued on. Lenz began to ordain his students as "Buddhist monks" in a quickie thumb-pressed-on-forehead ceremony, and relocated them to various cities to teach meditation and to advertise these courses with flyers for free-of-charge "Zen meditation" classes. And though Lenz's name was excluded from the flyers, frequent references to "my enlightened teacher" by the meditation instructor proved an effective recruiting tool.

By 1991, Lenz was encouraging students to secure high-ranking positions by way of occultism, or if that failed, to lie on their résumés, ascribing names of other students as false references (*Consultants and Contractors*, a trade magazine, kept a running tally of employers who'd been fooled into hiring Lenz's followers, otherwise known as "the California Raisins"). Lenz, who at the time owned estates in New Mexico, New York, and Long Island and drove seven cars, including three Mercedes and two Porsches, explained to his students that without a career trajectory that included a plan toward ever-ascending financial success, they would be uniformly kicked out, no exceptions.

Lenz's seminars filled venues from Alice Tully Hall in New York to the Starlight Ballroom at the Miramar Sheraton in Santa Monica. After seminars, Lenz took his followers to all-night raves with laser shows at the Rainbow Room. He would arrive with three or four women, hired for the evening from an escort service. Often they danced to the music of KMFDM or Ministry in a frenzied bump-and-grind. His female disciples wore evening gowns and heavily applied makeup by Shiseido; their faces had been washed with Basis soap and moisturized by Complex Routine, their hair conditioned by Nexxus. The men arrived in traditional black tie by Armani. There were no drinks provided, so students brought their own bottles of Jolt cola and Evian, often accompanied by bags of M&M's.

These brand names and labels were specifically sanctioned by Lenz. He regarded them as "high-vibe," which meant that they maximized occult powers and warded off psychic attacks. Yoplait yogurt and Mercedes 300 were high-vibe (Mercedes 400 and 500 models were apparently so high-vibe that they could only be driven by Lenz), as were Hot Chillys long-underwear, margaritas, Versace clothing, and Jif peanut butter. Skippy Crunchy was to be avoided in the face of grim consequences. Calistoga water and clothes by Calvin Klein were "low-vibe" brands. And when one was confronted with a particularly obstinate lower occult force, Lenz considered molasses poured into a jar of Jif and eaten with a spoon to be a source of psychic immunization. Lenz claimed that without the use of a spoon the potent blend would be undermined.

Animals were ranked according to vibe status as well—Scottish terrier dogs were highest of all. Lenz claimed that his dog, Vayu, had been a sacred warrior in another life and was one of the seven enlightened beings still alive. He said that in order for Vayu to maintain his enlightened state, students were to ignore him when he'd sidle up to them during seminars. Otherwise, he said, their low-vibe energy would permanently mar the animal.

"I've maintained for a long time that Lenz was a very lonely, depressed person," says Kaplan. "He had no one to relate to but his dog." Kaplan remembers receiving a late-night telephone call from Lenz, who wanted to share "a pearl of wisdom that Vayu just told me." Intended to be understood as a Zen koan, the statement went: "Meat is it."

By 1996, his book, *Surfing the Himalayas,* a ghostwritten account of an American snowboarder who embarks on a spiritual journey with Master Fwap, a Buddhist monk in Nepal, was being published by Warner Books, who gave Lenz a $250,000 advance and saw *Surfing* as the next *Celestine Prophecy,* but who later cancelled the deal due to Lenz's notoriety. St. Martin's Press picked up the book; blurbed by Laurie Anderson, Mary McFadden, and

Chicago Bulls coach Phil Jackson, it had a brief stint on the best-seller list.

For the book, Lenz was said to have spent as much as $1.5 million of his own money for full-page ads in *Rolling Stone* and *Sports Illustrated* and ads projected onto seventeen hundred multiplex screens around the country. *Newsweek* called the book "vapid," the review detailing, above all else, the exploitation of Lenz's followers. *Surfing* came to be seen as a cult recruiting tactic, though Lenz continued to trumpet the book as a *Jonathan Livingston Seagull* of the nineties. His follow-up endeavor, *Snowboarding to Nirvana*, a highly sexed and even more sensationalized version of its predecessor, was ignored by reviewers. A typical passage reads, "As she opened her legs a little wider I thrust more deeply into her. We kissed, and then everything went white. I don't remember much of what happened after that, except for the two of us passing through countless cascading dimensions of color and ecstasy."

In a last dire attempt to gain publicity, Lenz approached *Dateline* to do a segment on him. Their investigative piece only further unveiled Lenz's profligate dealings; this last tarnish to his image and final rebuff by mainstream culture left him despondent. During interviews, Lenz stopped referring to himself as Rama or alluding to his spiritual teaching. He called himself a "world-class author" who had been brutalized by the media (oddly, Lenz was named one of the "100 Smartest New Yorkers" in 1995 by *New York* magazine). "Oh, right. I'm a cult leader. What are you going to do? Put me in a boxcar, ship me off and gas me?" Lenz said during one of his last interviews. "Now, damn it! I am a hard-working guy. I love life. I love my family. I love my country. I am the victim."

In the middle of Lenz's book tour came a devastating blow. Vayu died. Stunned, Lenz watched his dog decompose on his living-room couch for three days. He canceled his remaining engagements and went into seclusion.

"That was a pretty dark time," one follower recalled. "After Vayu died, for months all Lenz talked about was how much pain he was in and how badly we were all fucking up." And though after a while Lenz resumed his comedy routines (of which no one who was questioned could remember a single humorous remark he ever made), he was said to have lost his usual "California dude stride." His stance suggested a weariness, his face became an inscrutable screen. He didn't monologue about "The Island" anymore, either. "The Island," at one time the only foreseeable sanctuary, was to have had high-vibe five-star hotels, an Ashram, a runway, and boating docks. "It was our big dream, our goal. We'd all live happily ever after," said this follower, who was making $200,000 a year and giving $84,000 of it to Lenz. He stopped paying, however, when Lenz, who continued to charge a monthly tuition of $7,000, created a new format in which his seminars were replaced by telepathic meetings that involved no direct contact. "I don't do cult without cult leader," this follower said. When asked if "cult" was the appropriate terminology for Lenz's group of adherents, he remarked, "Of course it was a fucking cult. We were a group of people following one individual. But it was a good cult."

In the years since Lenz's death, the stage has been set for a replacement in Lenz's absence. Three of his students—David Ash, a computer consultant living in New York, Roger Cantu, a Dallas meditation teacher, and Tony Chester, currently in Los Angeles, are all vying to establish themselves as Lenz's successor. The majority of his students have been contacted by them, and word has it that one of the aforementioned, who is offering seminars in "power golf," is a shoe-in for the next title.

Lenz's followers believe that their teacher's coup de grace was a fitting fuck you to the press, the perfect rhetorical flourish for all those who made his life an insurmountable hell. They believe, and maybe are slightly relieved, that there will be no miracle of resurrection this time, and that Lenz has, at last, made it to Nirvana. One follower recalls a quote from the Bhagavad Gita that, he says, is the embodiment of his teacher, whom he still refers to as Buddha: "Hell has three doors: lust, rage, and greed. And the man who learns to pass the three doors finds his own salvation."

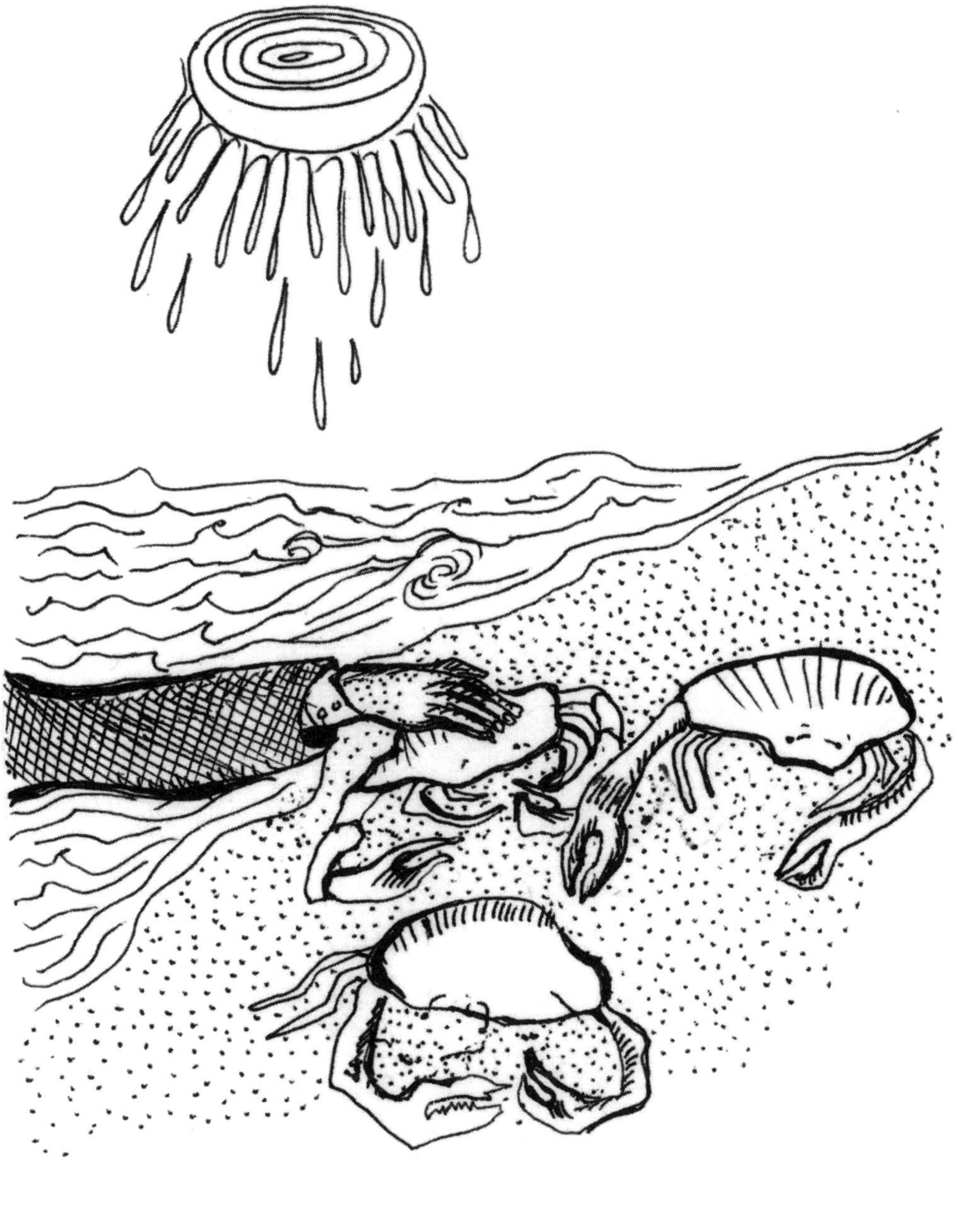

"Touches me but may have been accident
Was reaching for cutlery"
(Bao, page 137)

Silhouettes

A Project for *Open City* by Elliott Puckette

Adam Fuss, 1994

Alexandra Brown, 1995

Elliott Puckette, 1995

Liliane de Rothschild, 1996

Christopher Mason, 1995

Danny Moynihan, 1994

Louise Neri, 1995

Stephen Morrow, 1993

**"Would Kleenex
come under
Paper Products,
or Cosmetics?"**
(Skinner, page 69)

Postwar

Joyce Johnson

THERE WAS ONE THING ABOUT OUR HOUSE I COULD NEVER understand—why you could never hear a car turning in off the road, rolling to a stop in the grass. It must have been the trees, the way they absorbed sound, then reflected it. Shots would be fired in the woods; you never knew whether they were near or far. Or a wave of voices would drift over but you couldn't make out the words. Cars passed on our road at the rate of one every half hour, and if a driver got out and slammed the door, it was no more than a disturbance of the air. Soon you might hear steps on the back porch, find a face peering in at you through the little diamond-shaped window. For years I lived without locks. Now I have a doorman who buzzes visitors in, not that I have a steady stream. I get warned when someone's coming.

Up there on East Hill, it was usually a neighbor, occasionally a lost tourist, or a lister to ask if we'd made any improvements. Jehovah's Witnesses also turned up; it always amused me to offer them coffee. I never felt scared except in hunting season or those times in the seventies when certain visitors passed through and we had to be on the lookout for the feds.

The diamond-shaped window had old wavy glass, which made for weird first impressions. The reporter's face seemed a moon—all fleshy cheeks and big round lenses, tiny eyes. I opened the door and saw a big sandy-haired man, quite dressed up according to our local standards—everything new looking, well pressed, immaculate despite the heat. I wasn't in the mood for company, to put it mildly.

"Yes?" I said. "Looking for someone?" I was holding a couple of chipped green plates I'd decided to get rid of, the ones we'd eaten eggs off every morning. I'd been dismantling the kitchen, throwing out more than I was taking. It was the week I was clearing out for good.

He said he was looking for Patsy Straus, and I said, "Why?"

"Just to talk, ask a few questions." He had a boy's smile, though his eyes were really narrow. He started to explain that he was a reporter.

"Wait a minute," I said, and I stepped back into the house. I remember putting the two plates down on the kitchen sink and seeing my face shiny and streaked with dirt in the little mirror I'd left hanging. I let the cold water run, splashed it over my cheeks and neck before I went back out onto the porch. He was standing where I'd left him, staring at the garden. It was all delphiniums and foxgloves and those opium poppies with the blue-black centers. The delphiniums were collapsing every which way. I hadn't bothered to stake them that summer, hadn't even weeded much. "I'm Patsy Straus," I said.

He turned to look at me—taking his time, I thought, so he could add up his mental notes. An abandoned woman, a neglected garden—I could imagine a smart reporter making that connection. I was even wearing one of Alex's old blue shirts—not that he would have known—tied at the waist. It would have rounded out the image.

"How do you get all that stuff to grow?" he asked me. "How do you get the colors to come out right?"

I said, "Look, don't assume you're going to get me into any conversation." I paused and took a breath. "You want to know about Alex Hazen, right? Celine Chapman—"

"How do you know what I'm going to ask?"

"Other people have come by."

"I've seen poppies like that before," he said, "fields of them. It's quite a sight."

"Yes," I said. "They're Asiatic. You'll find a lot of them around here. The seeds get passed around."

"I saw them in Laos," he said, his eyes on mine. "But never since."

I said, "Look. I don't even know who you are."

By this time I was thinking he could be an agent, though the war had been over nearly five years. The feds used to drive up and down our road in pickup trucks, turn up at our parties in brand new overalls, a little over-friendly and enthusiastic, bringing their own six-packs of beer. "We're running out, man," Alex would say; he'd clap them on the shoulder. They were always happy to go for more. One guy was even pretty good at playing the guitar. So now a "reporter" was being sent instead. It figured.

"Jacob Bender," he said, easy about it as if I'd never warned him off, "from the *Boston Globe.*"

He took out his wallet and had me look at some press passes with his picture on them. Then he said, "Would you like to have my card?" I shook my head because I didn't really want it. What would I need it for? But he pressed one into the palm of my hand. "Keep it," he said, and I stuck it in the pocket of my old Indian cotton skirt and didn't throw it out until I did the wash in the city.

"So?" he said. "You're sure you're not going to change your mind?"

"Certain," I said.

He told me he'd driven from the airport in Burlington, gotten directions to the house from some woman in the post office, then totally lost his way driving around in the woods on our hill. I said I was sorry he'd gone to so much trouble for nothing. I really felt a little sorry for him.

"You wouldn't have a glass of water?" he asked. "I didn't think it would be so hot up here. Look at all the dust on that car."

"It needs to rain."

I told him he could come in for a minute. You couldn't turn someone away without water. That was something I'd learned when I first moved to the country. That when anyone showed up you dropped everything, whatever you were doing, and gave them your full attention for as long as they needed it. Even if you were expected somewhere else, you'd call up and say, "A neighbor's here," and the other party would understand perfectly. It was because we all depended on each other.

I asked him, "Do you want water? Or would you rather have iced tea?" Not that he was a neighbor, of course. He wanted tea. I poured him a glass and one for myself.

He gulped his drink, slouching against the refrigerator. The kitchen had originally been a shed, and this was where the roof slanted drastically. It had never bothered me or Alex. But this man took up a lot more room. There was barely an inch between the top of his head and the ceiling. I said, "Sit down if you want." Most of my stuff had already been sold. In the kitchen there was one remaining ailing chair. I'd bought it at a barn sale for a dollar; it still had all its original peeling blue paint. He gave it a quizzical glance and seated himself, brushing a couple of blue flakes off a leg of his spotless khakis.

"It'll hold you," I said. "It's stronger than it looks."

"And are you?" he asked in a funny, low voice.

I said, "What? Pardon me?" I didn't think I'd heard him right.

"Thanks for the chair."

I remember keeping busy for a while wrapping newspaper around cups. Every now and then I'd glance at him over my shoulder. I noticed his glass becoming empty by degrees; then all the yellow tea was gone and I expected him to get up and leave. But he seemed in no hurry, staring all around, as if the cracks in the old siding, the knotholes in the floorboards, might tell him something.

I knew it was just about four, although the electric clock was already in a box, and I wasn't keeping track of time. But the light in the kitchen had suddenly become perfectly balanced, the way it only was around that hour on summer afternoons, given enough sun streaming in from east and west, where the windows lined up with each other. Maybe that was the secret of the whole effect, why every board became infused with that soft gold, why even some promise of absolute harmony seemed to be offered. I suddenly had the clearest memory of walking in with Alex one August day twelve years before and finding the place golden and empty the way it was now and both of us knowing we wanted to live there before we even said a word to each other. Look no further, was what we both instantly thought. It's strange to think that light could have such power, that it could determine the direction of lives.

"I like your house," I heard the reporter say.

I said, "Yeah, I liked it, too."

"So why are you moving?"

I told him the truth, "Because I can't be happy here anymore," feeling a little surprised, as if somehow a lot of steps had just been skipped.

"I was in Seattle last week," he said.

"Oh?" I felt wary again now that he'd brought up Seattle.

"Spent a couple of days following Alex around. It wasn't his idea that I come up here and talk to you. Is Alex for real?" he asked me.

I said quickly, "Yes. Yes he is."

"So you're still a loyalist."

"I don't know what you'd call me. But I don't like labels much. Don't call me a loyalist in your article."

He asked if he could quote me on that, and I reminded him that this wasn't an interview.

He got up from the blue chair and came toward me. "Could I have one more glass of tea—for the road?"

I swung away from him, yanked open the refrigerator door, and grabbed at the half-gallon jar on the top shelf. It slipped from my fingers and crashed to the floor and I stepped backward against him, yelling, "Oh damn! Damn!" I remember feeling shocked by the warmth of his body, the smell of the soap his shirt had been washed in. He put one hand down on my shoulder. "Hey, you don't have shoes." There was glass and spilt tea all around our feet. I didn't move for a moment or so. When he took his hand away, I could still feel its weight. It had been about two years since anyone had touched me.

"Tell me where your broom is. I'm good at floors," he said.

I was thirty-six and pretty well leveled. By the time I grew out of Alex, I'd be old, I thought. When Alex was leaving, he said we'd always be part of each other's lives. Of course that couldn't be so. I could no longer feel him in my life at all, though he was huge as an absence, a void that sat across from me at the kitchen table, followed me up the stairs, woke me in the mornings earlier than I wanted to be conscious with the sky still dark. I'd take the radio out of the kitchen each night, carry it up to put beside my bed. I'd reach for the switch as soon as my eyes opened and catch the end of Music through the Night. Music didn't help me; it was voices I was starved for. I'd feel better when the news came on.

It's not a good idea to go on living where you used to be happy. Most people don't get to be happy for ten years. Alex and I never believed that marriage was necessary, and I still don't think much of the whole institution. We decided it would be selfish to have children, not wishing to add to the pollution and overcrowdedness of the world. He used to call me his running mate. In the first years we did run together—to Alaska, to Mexico, New Orleans—then we drove up to Vermont and found the house, which was a wreck we had to rebuild, knowing nothing of such matters, and we settled down. It was the first time in my life I had ever felt at home.

We had no money to speak of, so I kept discovering ways of being capable—ways of being indispensable, or so I thought—while Alex theorized and wrote and organized. I could make an extensive list of the things I learned to do—I can break down a car engine, raise chickens, shingle a wall, grow a quarter acre of strawberies, put up forty quarts of tomatoes. I can chop down a tree and shoot a porcupine if necessary; I can drive a truck downhill on black ice. I can look innocent and respectable and get someone across the border. None of these skills are the slightest use to me now.

"This is my little sister," I told people in town when Celine was sent to us. As her belly got bigger, she looked more and more childlike herself with that cropped pale hair and those enormous blue eyes behind the granny glasses that did very little to disguise her. A soft girl who once drove a truck full of stolen explosives. Almost single-handedly I delivered her baby because we were afraid of the questions they might ask at the hospital. She left him with us after she turned herself in. Oh yes, if a mother was needed, I could even do the mother thing.

About a week before the reporter showed up, I woke up later than usual one morning and switched Alex on in the middle of a sentence just as if I'd summoned him. That voice of his was right there in the room with me, warm and enthusiastic as ever, talking about the big protest that was going to shut down the nuclear submarine plant on the Coast, about activists pouring in from all over the country. I lay there at first as if someone had hit me on the head with a brick. At one point the interviewer said patronizingly, "Sounds like you're nostalgic for the sixties."

As usual, Alex didn't miss a beat. "Nostalgia is a waste of time when you're trying to change the way things are right now." The answer struck me as pompous. I wondered whether some shift was finally going on inside my brain, because nothing Alex said had ever sounded so pompous to me. I yelled back at the radio that he had a hell of a lot to be nostalgic for.

I braced myself to hear him say, "Celine. . .Celine and I," so I could measure the level of his happiness. Maybe he'd talk to his listeners about how he believed Celine was purer than he was, about what it meant to have the courage to go beyond theory, and how for three years the letters had gone back and forth and he'd held her hand in the visitors' room at the prison and promised to wait for her. I knew everything about that voice on the air, all its secret modulations, its funny flattened *a*s, that speaker's trick of going suddenly from soft to loud that could move a whole crowd to the edge of their chairs. . .

"Is it his words?" the reporter asked me as he swept the glass toward the dustpan. "Or is it the delivery?"

I remember getting hot in the face. I told him I still hadn't figured out the answer to that question.

"I'd say it's the delivery. I transcribed a couple of his speeches that I heard. On the page, there's no magic."

"I'm not the right person to ask, you know," I said. "I don't want to be tearing him down."

"Wow," he laughed, leaning the broom against the wall. "I'd like you to feel that way about me if I broke up with you."

"I'll never feel that way about anyone again."

I took a sponge from the sink and started mopping the tea off the floor. Any minute now he'll go, I thought. But he stayed where he was, watching me as I straightened up and squeezed out the sponge.

"You haven't said where you're moving to."

"New York." I told him my mother had died and I'd decided to take over her apartment.

"And the house? What's going to happen to it after you leave?"

"I'm selling it," I told him.

"Really?" He sounded surprised. "You're sure you want to sell a place like this?"

"I could never live here again."

"Your feelings could change," he said.

"If I didn't sell it, I'd always feel pulled back here. I know that wouldn't do me any good."

"You have a buyer?" he asked me.

"Not yet. The Realtor will take care of that."

He walked back to where he'd sat and started looking around the kitchen again. There was a little breeze outside; you could hear the leaves on the silver birch stirring and rippling. The shafts of light still spilling in were making all the strawberry preserves in the mason jars flash like garnets. He said in an almost embarrassed way, "I know someone who might be interested."

"To live here year round or just to have a summer place?"

He thought for a moment, then answered, "Just somewhere to get away to. Whenever."

"Sounds like you wouldn't mind that yourself."

"Maybe," he said, still embarrassed for some reason. "Maybe I'd get into the quiet. My friend is the one who talks about becoming a country person."

"You prefer cities."

"I've moved around all my life. I don't know what I prefer."

I said I'd write down the Realtor's number for his friend. "I'm trying not to get involved much in the sale. I want it to happen fast, that's all."

"You could get burned that way," he said. "Would you show me around? Or is that something you'd rather not do?"

I wondered for a moment, Was he still after his story? Was this a way to trick me into saying more than I wanted? "You're sure you have this friend?"

"No lie," he said, grinning. "But why should you trust me?"

I wasn't like Alex, decisive and single-minded when he wanted to move on to what he called "a different phase" after Celine came out of jail and picked up the kid. I'd spent the summer saying goodbye to the house in mournful stages with every picture

I took down from a wall, every book I put into a box. My friend Cynthia suggested a yard sale after she'd given up trying to convince me to stay on. We'd always joked to each other that if one of us ever dropped dead, the death would be followed by the yard sale of the century. I'd finally had one at the end of July, tried to make it into a party with a keg of beer, pitchers of iced tea and lemonade. It looked like my whole life turned inside out—all the furniture standing in the long grass, rocking chairs set amongst daisies and self-heal, my yellow Victorian settee with the busted springs under the apple tree, bees buzzing against the screened sides of the baby crib. All the stuff that had somehow accumulated, despite our original beliefs in the holiness of owning nothing.

I was the hopeless accumulator, the one with the subversive impulse to make things pretty. Alex had no use for pretty. He let me win at least half the battles about what came into the house, but he gave me a hard time about my flower garden. Real Vermonters, he used to point out, mostly grew what was edible, though there might be some daylilies around a foundation that would more or less take care of themselves, or a lilac tree planted a hundred years ago. My pink tulips and violet campanula were suburban, signs of conspicuous consumption. Alex's mother adored gardening; he'd grown up in Greenwich, always hated mowing the grass, hated the flagstone pathway to the front door lined with military rows of red and white petunias, hated the wall-to-wall carpeting inside that oppressed him as much as the perfect lawn. I loved him for all the things he hated, but I kept planting my flowers.

It was a sensational yard sale. People brought their kids and their dogs, and the kids wandered off to pick raspberries, and the sky darkened and rain spattered down, but no one left because they knew the sun would be out five minutes later. It was one of those days when each new cloud brought a different weather. Cynthia took me by the elbow and murmured, "Let's go smoke a joint," pulling me behind the house and into the pines. We sat on a log for a while, dropping ashes onto the damp moss, not saying much in the dark hush of the trees. She peered into my eyes when we were through. "Feel any better now?"

"I thought I was doing great," I said. "Life of the party."

"Not quite. Not quite, dolling." The way she said *dolling* always killed me. "I'll have to get me a new co-conspirator, I guess," she said sadly. We used to have fun flouting our men every once in a while, driving around the state together in search of exotic perennials in distant nurseries.

I went back to the yard sale feeling floaty and weightless, and began letting people drive away with the most outrageous bargains. I remember selling someone Alex's annotated copy of *Growing Up Absurd* for a nickel. By the time everyone went home, only the settee was left. I left it out under the apple tree, let the rain fall on it and the field mice carry away the stuffing. It was still out there when the reporter came.

It was a stripped house I showed him, vibrating like a drum. You could hear every creak, every step we took. I was used to the sounds of my own feet; his made a huge racket going up the stairs behind me. Our voices bounced off the walls of the empty bedrooms. In the one where Celine had slept, which we later fixed up for the child, there were nothing but bedsprings and a Matchbox car on the windowsill. I still couldn't bear to go in there. "A baby was born right here," I said. If he hadn't been a reporter, that was the moment I might have told him everything. Sometimes the only people you can talk to are the ones you think you'll never see again.

"Celine's kid?" he was quick to ask.

"Well, you know all about it then," I said, walking out onto the landing to wait for him. I shut the door again as soon as he came out.

He took off his glasses and wiped them on his sleeve; he looked younger without them. "Anything you want to add?" I wondered if his way of being gentle with a person was to sound completely offhanded.

I shook my head. "Better not to."

He could have pressed me but he didn't. Instead he said, "So what's left up here? The master bedroom?"

I'd saved it for last. There were piles of clothes and papers all over the floor and as usual I hadn't bothered to make the bed. I really didn't want him going in there. It didn't have much to do with the state of the room. The truth was, I hadn't yet found out how I'd be in my new life, what I'd do if a man made a move. I often felt I'd forgotten everything I once knew about men and women, that if I ever went to bed with anyone it would be like losing my virginity all over again. Alex had somehow left me sealed.

I stood in the doorway and let the reporter go in by himself. The shades were down and the pillows were still bunched up and the sheets were twisted halfway off the mattress, but at least they were clean and white.

A stranger could do it, I told myself. Break the seal.

He gave the bed a glance, then stepped over a pile of jeans and nightgowns and walked over to the windows. "There's no view here," he said after he'd pulled up the shades. "There is one," I said. "The apple tree."

"A tree isn't what I'd call a view. Besides, it makes everything dark. These branches are practically growing in."

"Well, someone planted it about a hundred years ago."

"I'd want to wake up and look straight across to the hills."

"You can do that in the other rooms," I told him. "You should see it in the fall, full of little gold apples. Very good for cooking."

"I'm not cut out to be a tree saver. I like a bedroom bright."

"What about your friend?" I asked him. We seemed to have forgotten about his friend, the friend who wanted to be a country person, as if you could just buy the right place and make yourself into one.

"My friend might go for the apples. You never know."

He'd started walking toward me, but then he paused and put a hand on one of the pine bedposts. "This is a terrific bed, by the way. You're not leaving this behind?"

"I'm throwing it in," I said.

He stood there rubbing the wood with his thumb. He had a heavy plaited silver ring on one finger. His nails were clipped straight across.

I wondered what I'd do if he were my lover, if I'd chop down the tree because he asked me to. I thought of us rolling in my tangled sheets, the weight of him, his mouth all over mine, how his neck might smell of laundry soap. I wouldn't, I told myself. I'd hold out.

"So you're interested in the house," I said.

"You know what I wanted?" he said with a laugh. "I wanted to get us up here."

I thought about the reporter's friend, how she must have said goodbye to him so innocently that morning. She was in the room with us as he came forward with the smile that had always charmed her. But I didn't stop him once he'd touched me. I felt pitiless, really.

"You're my oven. What makes you so warm?" Alex used to whisper in the bed I was about to leave behind. When his mind filled up with Celine, I couldn't tell the difference. I could still just float away on my stupid happiness.

Letters

Takeover Indication

I didn't even have to open my last issue of *Open City* [Number Seven] to discover that this, what I once thought of as one of the last bastions of true literary culture, had embarked upon a similar road as mainstream media. As Tina Brown's forthcoming *Talk* magazine has aligned itself with the film industry, *Open City* has done the same thing with Indie Rock. The same sort of male-dominated, hegemonic, one-culture-under-one-supposedly-for-all strategy that has seeped its way into commercial publishing (also indicated by the recent Bertelsmann takeover of Random House) has infiltrated a nonprofit so-called literary venture. I just hope my next issue does not arrive emblazoned with the new title: *Open Synergy*.

A concerned reader in Queens

Uncle Ryan in Chicago

Dear Thomas,

I received your letter on Wednesday, Febuary 17th. I was very happy that you replied, because I didn't really expect anyone to answer. I enjoyed your influential words, which will stick with me during my travels in pursuing writing as a career. Thank you.

I called Ryan, the Chicago writer you suggested to me, and we talked for a couple of hours. I met him the next day at a place called the Earwax Café, which was interesting because neither of us knew what the other looked like. We found each other though, and talked for a little bit and we both ordered black English Breakfast tea, and then went to some local bookstores and record stores. We talked about everything, but I couldn't help but feel as though he was an uncle figure I was sent to visit by my parents. "Damian, you'll like your uncle Ryan. He'll show you around town." My mind exaggerates situations, sorry.

We talked about writing, and he reminded me to pick up your literary publication, which I picked up that day, *Open City* Number Six. We also spent time rummaging through used records and CDs, where I found two cheap used Pavement singles. Ryan told me that you enjoyed the poetic lyrics and diverse sounds of Pavement as well (I need to pick up the *Open City* with an entry by Steve Malkmus). When we went to the bookstore we saw a little bit of everything, from the classics, to the Beat generation, to Crispin Glover's book *Rat Catching* (it's not just a clever name, oh no, it's actually about the art of rat catching!!). We laughed talking about how Crispin once tried to kick David Letterman while on his show. I also talked to him about your relationship, and how that began.

"Normally we get Mercedes, BMWs, Lexuses, things like that, but one day this guy pulls up in this old green car with leather seats. Gets out wearing something like a T-shirt, all unshaven, not the type I usually see. So I help him get his bags out, and I see that he's got a Pavement CD in his trunk, so I ask him what he did. He answered sheepishly, 'I'm a writer.' I answered him back, 'I'm a writer, too.' And it was strange, because about two weeks earlier I had picked up my first copy of *Open City*, and I was telling all my friends about it, telling them to buy it, and here was the editor. I told him I had just ordered a subscription and out of nowhere he gives me this great big bear hug! That's the kind of guy he is...So him and this other guy named Robert Bingham go up to their room. Later on I have to get something from their car, something they forgot, and I go up to their room, and it's a mess. Clothes everywhere, beer bottles everywhere, Pavement blasting—both of them sitting there with their shirts off! It was a bit shocking, because no one ever did things like that in the hotel."

We walked back to Ryan's apartment, which was empty since his girlfriend was in California. He gave me a tour, adding colorful comments such as "See that wet towel lying on the side of the tub?" and "See those dirty socks?" followed by an apologetic, "They wouldn't be there if my girlfriend was here." He was going out to see a favorite Irish band later on that night, so he dropped me off at the train station. I thanked him and took the train home...that was tonight.

Thank you for introducing me to a local writer. It felt really good to be around another person with such an enjoyment of literature. I thought I would find these people at this college, but I haven't yet, so his company was refreshing. I hope to keep in contact with him...thanks again.

Damian Manire
Chicago, Illinois

P.S. Tell Robert Bingham I enjoyed his essay "Soft Money," and his "limousine liberals." I will be picking up his book when I get through the ton of books I have to finish (including one of your favorites, *Nine Stories.* Ryan showed me your introduction to *Seduction Theory*).

Waiting for the Primaries

Now that no one reads much of anything, never mind literary magazines, what is *Open City* going to do with itself?

Molly Bloomberg
Lebanon, New Hampshire

The Euro

Dear Adrian Dannatt,
Nice to hear from you. I do remember you of course—my brush with the world of the international literary éclat! So you can depend upon it that the mention of Alistair Brotchie of Atlas Press being intrigued by my magazine, *Otis Rush,* was very good for my spirit.

Open City looks good. I've dipped into it a few times. The girl with the big nose, whose mouth pleases men (not Monica, but a poet early in the mag [Deborah Garrison]) was being unduly hard on herself I hope. I liked her poems. The "handsome pants" story (or were they "lucky pants"?) I liked though the underpants-and-portraits art idea was too too twee. (There's a guy in Adelaide photographing the penises of all the men he gets off with—sort of like John Rechy's *Numbers*). Pointless rigor. Demonstrating the downside of Kosuth's (or Sol LeWitt's) notion that when you get an idea, follow it through without deviating, don't compromise halfway though. Okay if you've never had a bad idea. I'm writing without *Open City* before me: There were other things I liked in it and much I haven't gotten to.

I actually mention Michael Brownstein [from *Open City* Number Four] in a couple of poems. I love his book *Country Cousins* and have sold considerable numbers in my shop over the years—all by personal recommendation. One of my partner's sons read it over Xmas and snorted and yelped all the way.

I got to Paris and bits of North Italy in 1994. My partner Cath Kennealy was part of Jacques Rancourt's Anglo-French poetry conference. I carried her bags. I tried your phone number once or twice, but to no avail. I figured you might be jet-setting.

I was in New York for two and a half days—and didn't call; there wasn't time. We had dinner with Tony Towle, though, another hero of mine—who thoroughly lived up to my exalted ideas of him. We met Harry Mathews in Paris (and Siena). He too was admirable and impressive.

Your lawyer friend, John Friedland, seemed rather driven—and I wasn't (though not for that reason) able to spend a lot of time with him. He bought me drinks that I should've bought him and we discussed Walter Benjamin, Marshall Berman, world affairs, and the sadly marginal status Australia has in his eyes—and much more probably.

He said you might be seeking John Forbes's last book. Let me know and where I should send it in return for *Open City*.

Ken Bolton
The Experimental Art Foundation
Adelaide, Australia

Fire in Detroit

Dear Tom,

You asked how things are going.

I'm back working seventy hours a week on my job in the import business, after a short break.

There was a fire in my building the night after the Super Bowl. I was passed out drunk. The landlady, a loud-voiced black woman, ran down the halls pounding on doors to wake people up. I heard her as a distant dream, and tried to ignore her. Then I smelled smoke.

We make plans about what we'll take in an emergency. I might've wanted to take my wallet, books, and a past manuscript. Something impelled me to just get out of there. I grabbed jeans, shoes, and a jacket, nothing else.

Thick clouds of smoke rushed down the hallways as I ran outside.

We stood in the cold and snow for two hours as the fire department did their thing. No one had carried possessions. The landlady wore a T-shirt, cutoffs, and sandals, and was shivering.

"I guess I can go to work," I said.

"I don't have anyplace to go," she told me.

When the fire was out I went back in for clothes. An apartment building is eerie after a fire. The place was soaked with dripping water. At the same time lingered the smoke and smell.

I remained there the next night, coughing out my guts. The smell made me sick to my stomach, as if I'd eaten a pot of burnt popcorn. Electricity worked intermittently. It was out when I arrived home and I had to feel my way up the stairs and down the hall. When the lights went on I ran the taps. Dark brown water came from them.

There was no heat. I was feverish and thought I was dying. I opened a window to air out the place, but in came the cold. In the morning I left.

I stayed first at a buddy's place. Bob's a retired customs inspector. He was glad to have me. I was supposed to sleep on his sofa. We stayed up late watching boring Truffaut movies on a Canadian TV station. I was sick and exhausted, my eyes closed, head rocking back and forth on my neck. Bob continued talking.

"Yeah, my accountant cost me five hundred bucks on my income tax!" Eventually I passed out. The TV set might still be on.

I moved on to my brothers, from the old inspector to the old soldier. My brother had been a sergeant in the army (Airborne). He ran his place the same way. He forced me to take cough medicine every three hours on the dot, whether I wanted to or not. At 1800 hours it was time for my shower. He pointed to his watch.

I said, "I don't want to take a shower."

"I've already got the towels laid out!"

My brother is a hard-core member of A.A. Religious pamphlets were placed strategically around my room. One evening he had some of his A.A. friends over. His girlfriend, another fanatic, cooked dinner. My brother moved his dilapidated guests around like chess pieces. "Tom, you sit here. Barb, you sit over there." The conversation centered around which of the several meetings in the area they would attend, and how everyone would get there, as many didn't drive. They had replaced an obsession with the bottle with an obsession with A.A.

My only thought was that I needed a beer.

When I couldn't take anymore I went back to the doomed apartment building in a doomed neighborhood. After three weeks the heat came back. Half the residents are gone. Paint is falling off the walls in the halls and stairwells, but the smoke smell is gradually dying.

I'm looking for another building to move to, or another city.

Karl Wenclas
Detroit, Michigan